THE HOLE IN THE WALL

– J.B. AND THE PIRATES –

TAMI HRITZAY

 INFINITY
PUBLISHING

Copyright © 2013 by Tami Hritzay

ISBN 978-0-7414-8266-2
Library of Congress Control Number: 2013900644

Printed in the United States of America

Published February 2013

INFINITY PUBLISHING
1094 New DeHaven Street, Suite 100
West Conshohocken, PA 19428-2713
Toll-free (877) BUY BOOK
Local Phone (610) 941-9999
Fax (610) 941-9959
Info@buybooksontheweb.com
www.buybooksontheweb.com

DEDICATION

This book is dedicated first to God for giving me the gift of life and creativity. To my parents who always encouraged me in whatever I did. To my students who have listened to my stories and inspired me to continue. To my "other" sister, Jean, thanks for editing and helping me accomplish this task. Dear little, T.P., thanks for reminding me of the simple joys of being a child. I'll always remember the barn tea party. And last but not least, to Charlie who lay on the floor begging to hear the rest of the story. It's here! Enjoy!

TABLE OF CONTENTS

THE ART ROOM SECRET

Gazing at the art room pictures, J.B. listened half-heartedly to Miss Plum until the jaguar blinked. His blue eyes widened. He rubbed them, then looked back at the picture. Again the great cat blinked. Mouth wide open in disbelief, J.B. sat transfixed by the sight.

"James Bud, are you going to spend the rest of the day in art class?" Ms. Plum's voice cut through the air, jolting J.B. back to reality and his eyes away from the pictures on the wall.

Turning his curly red head toward Ms. Plum, he stammered, "No, Ma'am." Hastily he jumped to his feet and glanced at his best friend, Wayne.

Wayne stared at him with his big brown eyes. "Are you O.K.? Your face is white, like you've seen a ghost! Even your freckles are pale."

"A ghost, yeah, sort of...." J.B. looked at the jaguar and nodded. "Jaguar."

"Jaguar? What about it?" asked Wayne as they fell in line to go back to their 4th grade room.

"It's eyes moved, like someone was watching us. I'll tell you more later," he muttered when they entered their homeroom.

J.B. sat rethinking the jaguar episode. Finally he glanced at the clock. Seconds away from dismissal, he had an idea.

RRRRing! The bell sounded and he jumped up, grabbing his backpack.

"Wait, J.B.," called Wayne.

"What?" He turned to face his sandy haired friend.

"I have to return my library books. Where are you going?" asked Wayne.

"To help my grandfather. You can catch up." He walked briskly out the door and sprinted down the darkened hallway toward the janitor's room. The door hung slightly ajar. J.B. quickly pushed it open. Taking a step, he accidently bumped the full pail of water near the door. The pail tipped, spilling water. He lost his footing and slid across the floor. His arm hit the table, knocking the leg loose and dumping the contents of the table on his head and the floor. A jackknife fell by his hand. He picked it up and smiled--his old knife. He thought he'd lost it. He slid it into his pocket.

"Ho....J.B...are you O.K.?" Mr. Hritzay, his grandfather, turned on the main light.

"Well, as O.K. as a wet hen," laughed J.B.

Giving him a hand, Mr. Hritzay pulled his grandson to his feet and patted him on the head. "Boys--always on some kind of adventure in their minds. You know, you should always be prepared for adventure, just in case."

"Sure, Gramps. Hey, you look tired. Do you need help cleaning today?" asked J.B.

"Did that bump on the head affect your mind?" laughed his grandfather. "You've never offered to help before. Are you in trouble or something?" Mr. Hritzay touched J.B.'s forehead. "Good, no fever," he laughed. "I can always use help. Why don't you help me set this table up and put all the things back on it?" Within minutes they had the table fixed and Gramps reached for the mop.

Running footsteps sounded outside the door. Wayne rushed into the room. Tripping over the now empty water pail, he slid on the wet floor, crashing into the wooden table. The table toppled over again, spilling the contents over the sprawled Wayne.

"Holy Moly, Wayne......are you O.K.?" Mr. Hritzay rushed over to him

J.B. stood, laughing. "Wayne, you just did a repeat of my trick....how did you know?"

Helping Wayne to his feet, Mr. Hritzay brushed his head and back. "Boys, I've had enough entertainment for today. I'm just glad you're both not hurt." Mr. Hritzay nodded to his grandson, "Take your buddy and go clean the art room. You need to be finished by 4:30. Sweep the floor, clean the desks, and don't play with the paper cutter. Got it?" Mr. Hritzay looked at both boys.

"Yes, sir," J.B. glanced at Wayne.

"Yes, Mr. Hritzay," Wayne replied.

J.B. stepped over to the door and quickly grabbed his backpack. "Until an adventure, Grandpa. See ya, Wayne!" he yelled and bolted down the hall.

Wayne darted out the door. "Later, Mr. Hritzay." Then he, too, sped down the hall.

"Kids, nowadays......in a hurry to go anywhere..." muttered Mr. Hritzay. He turned and walked down the opposite hall.

J. B. was first to reach the art room door. He dropped his backpack and ran to the jaguar picture on the wall.

His friend ran in to join him. "Oooh....J.B., he looks so scary!" mocked Wayne.

J.B. ignored the comment and started touching the picture. He touched the eyes and his fingers poked through the canvas into empty space. "There, I told you so." He looked triumphantly at Wayne. "There is a hole behind this painting. Someone was looking through the jaguar's eyes."

"So just what does that mean?" asked Wayne.

"I'm going to find out today!" vowed J.B. He stepped over to the closet door on the left side of the picture. Janking the door open, he could make out the two holes that lined up with the jaguar's eyes. Light from the art room filtered through to shine on the back wall of the closet like a lantern ray. He studied the wall and mindlessly started tapping on it. Tap...tap...tap... klunck.... klunck.

"Hear that?" J.B. asked his friend.

"Hear what?" asked Wayne.

"Listen...it sounds weird, like an echo." J.B. thumped the wall again. "Let's push it." He pushed against the closet's back wall. "Give me a hand." He motioned to his friend.

Wayne stood beside him and together the boys pushed. Nothing moved.

"Well, we pushed it...maybe it will slide," grunted J.B., unwilling to give up. Flattening his hands on the wall, he took a step forward. Shifting his body against the wall, he pushed harder. The wall groaned and started to slide to the right! A blast of air came through the foot wide opening. Papers blew off the side shelves.

"Oh, my goodness!" J.B. yelled. He waved his arm into the dark hole. "I feel wind!" He pulled his arm back and turned to Wayne. "That's sooo weird!"

"Yeah," agreed Wayne, "but look--that's even more weird." He pointed to the wall. The wall, the plain brown wall, appeared to be shimmering. Brilliant colors of red, green, and blue cascaded down the length of it. J.B. and Wayne stepped back in amazement.

The colors glowed, then started to separate, revealing a picture. The boys watched, wide-eyed as the image of a ship came into focus. The waters around the ship seemed to be moving, yet the ship remained poised and still.

"Wow! I never saw this before and Ms. Plum usually has us open this closet for more paper," sputtered Wayne.

"Yeah, and look," added J.B. pointing to the ship. "It's a pirate ship. There's the Jolly Roger flag. Hey! Look at that lantern on the deck. It's blinking green!"

"But this is a plain wall," muttered Wayne.

Wind blew through the hole ruffling the boys' hair.

J.B. sniffed the breeze. "Hey, what does that smell like?" He looked at Wayne.

His friend replied, "It smells like the ocean....it reminds me of when I went to Myrtle Beach. How about you?"

"Yeah," muttered J.B. "Funny thing, Wayne, we are miles from any water, much less an ocean!" Eyes narrowed, he looked at his watch. "It's 3:55. We have a few minutes to check it out before we clean. Let's see what is behind this wall," J.B., squeezed into the dark hole, disappearing from sight.

"Hey, wait for me!" cried Wayne. Then he too, slipped into the darkness.

2. BETWEEN TWO WORLDS

J.B. turned to Wayne. "Well, buddy, I want to find out where this leads. Are you coming?"

Wayne stared at the dark tunnel ahead. Suddenly he spoke, his voice trembling. "I don't know if we should go on. Maybe we'll run into whoever was looking through the jaguar's eyes. Maybe they're a criminal or something!"

J.B. glared at his friend. "Fine! Stay here. I'm going to get some answers. I don't care what you do. Are you scared of the dark, Mr. Boy Scout?"

"Quit making fun of me. Being a Boy Scout has nothing to do with the dark. I'm weighing out options. Boy Scouts plan; they don't rush into situations blindly, J.B." Wayne jumped out of the hole and leaned over a desk to grab his backpack. Opening a pocket he pulled out a flashlight. "I want to see where I'm walking."

"Sorry," apologized J.B., and together they stepped into the darkness, the ocean smells luring them on.

Wayne shined the light on the walls. The tunnel was about four feet wide and six feet tall. The beam of light spread twenty feet down the tunnel.

"Wow!" cried J.B. "Let's see how far it goes."

Carefully the boys walked down the tunnel. Shining the light to and fro, they studied the walls. Only the sound of their sneakered feet echoed in the darkness.

After walking about ten minutes, the boys stopped.

"Wayne," said J.B.," it usually doesn't take us 10 minutes to walk from the art room to the stairs. If this tunnel is in the walls, we should have already come to a turn or the end."

"You're right," agreed Wayne. No sooner had he spoken when the tunnel turned sharply to the right.

Rounding the corner, both boys saw a doorway ten feet away. Green lights blinked around the edge of the door. A single blinking green light glowed on the wall beside the door.

"Hey, what's that!" wondered J.B. He touched the light. Suddenly the lights changed color, this time blinking red. He touched it again. The lights changed to blue.

"Leave it alone!" yelled Wayne.

"O.K., don't touch," mumbled J.B. He grinned and touched the light once more. The lights returned to green. "There, are you happy, Wayne?"

His friend shook his head and put his flashlight in his pocket.

J.B. stepped closer to the portal. The green lights continued to blink. He reached out to touch the door. His hand went right through the door and disappeared! Startled, he jumped back, yanking his hand and shaking it.

"Did you see that!" he sputtered, looking at Wayne.

Wayne's brown eyes stared in astonishment. "Yeah....like it plain disappeared. Do it again," he told J.B.

Before he could put his hand back through the doorway, four numbers appeared floating in that space--one, seven, three, eight.

"Hey, is that a code or something?" wondered Wayne.

J.B. shook his head, "I don't know. Maybe it's a date. That would make it the year seventeen thirty-eight. I'm gonna try it again."

This time J.B. pushed his entire arm through up to his shoulder. It disappeared. Once he pulled his arm back, He turned to Wayne. "O.K., this time I'm stepping through.

Once I get through I'll yell to let you know I'm O.K., then you follow."

Wayne scowled. He looked at the blinking lights, then back to the red-headed boy. "What time is it, J.B.?"

"We're discovering something awesome and you're worried about time!" J.B. shook his head. "Well, yeah, I did tell Grandpa we'd get done by 4:30." He glanced at his watch. "It is 3:56--hmmm--maybe I need a new battery. We've got plenty of time, Wayne." He stood at the doorway. "I'm going through." Taking a deep breath, he stepped through the doorway.

Wayne watched as he disappeared into nothingness. "J.B.....J.B.....can you hear me!" Wayne yelled. He strained his ears to listen. No sound. Wayne yelled again, "J.B., it's not funny. Answer me, please!"

At last he heard his friend's voice. "Wayne, you're never going to believe this. Step through, now!"

Gulping, Wayne closed his eyes and slipped through the doorway. Wind blew on his face and the crash of waves jarred his senses. Opening his eyes he saw his friend, a beach, and the ocean in front of him.

J.B. ran over to him and slapped him on the back. "Boy, how do you like this surprise?"

"I-I don't believe this," Wayne stammered. "Hey look! What's that?" Wayne took a couple steps and picked up an object lying in the sand. "It's a leather pouch. Let's see what's in it." The leather was cracked and worn, but inside were papers fastened together with leather thongs.

J.B. noticed the numbers on the front. "Hey, look at the numbers--one, seven, three, eight. What is this?" He thumbed through the yellow sheets. "Whoever wrote this spells worse than we do!"

"Yeah," agreed Wayne, "and I thought I was bad."

J.B. tried to read one of the scrawled pages. "I wonder if this is someone's journal?" He looked again at the numbers on the front page. "Seventeen thirty-eight--this must be the year seventeen thirty-eight! We must have found a time portal! That's it, a time portal!" J.B. yelled and jumped up and down

"I didn't think they really existed," the sandy haired boy murmured. Looking at the beach and surf he smiled, "Catch me if you can!" Shoving the journal in his pocket, he touched J.B.'s shoulder and took off running along the beach.

J.B. followed in pursuit, running hard to catch up. "Tag, you're it!" he yelled, touching Wayne's back. Wayne stumbled and fell on the yellow sand. J.B. tripped and landed beside him.

Both boys rolled in the sand, laughing. Standing up, J.B. brushed the sand off his pants. He offered his hand to Wayne and pulled him up. Turning around, J.B. faced the ocean and brushed the sand off Wayne's back. "Oh my goodness!" he exclaimed. "Do you see what I see?"

Wayne turned around to face the ocean. His mouth dropped open. Anchored in the bay was a ship. What frightened both boys was the flag waving in the ocean breeze. The skull and cross bones....The Jolly Roger! "A Pirate ship.....cool!" cried Wayne.

"A Pirate ship means adventure," said J.B. "Maybe we'll see some pirates. Hey! We could fight them! Take that!" He jokingly poked Wayne with a stick.

Wayne grabbed the stick and yanked it, sending J.B. to the sand. J.B. jumped up, laughing. "Hey, what time is it now?" he asked Wayne.

Pulling out his cell phone, Wayne answered, "3:57. Hmm, time must go real slow here.""

"We still have some time to play," declared J.B. and he took off running toward the beach. Wayne ran after him. As they played in the sand, neither boy noticed the large figure hiding behind the palm tree.

The figure's eyes followed the boys' every movement. When the boys moved off the beach closer to the old palm tree, the figure crouched, trying to disappear.

J.B. stood in front of the tree. "Hey, Wayne, don't forget where the time portal is!" He stomped his foot in the sand. Moving closer to the palm he turned toward Wayne. "Wayne, look over here. I said don't forget where the time portal is!" J.B. saw a frightened look on Wayne's face.

Wayne yelled, "J.B.! Oh, good grief.....Pirates--watch out!"

J. B. was grabbed from behind, his arms pinned to his sides. Without thinking he bit with all his might on the hairy arm that held him!

"Aawww..." screamed the unknown attacker. In a rage, he threw J.B. back against the palm tree. The boy crumpled in a heap on the sand.

"You creep! Take this!" Wayne grabbed a stick and lunged with all his energy toward the pirate. The stick stopped. Wayne looked and saw a second pirate standing there. The pirate threw the stick and grabbed Wayne by his collar, holding him in mid air. "Let me go, you creeps! You killed my best friend!" Wayne kicked helplessly. The second pirate tightened his grip on Wayne's collar. The boy started to choke.

"Would you like to join your friend then?" the pirate laughed. "Well, Tall John, here's cabin boy number two."

Tall John suggested, "Hey, One Eye...let's take them back to the ship, after I get me talking pouch." With a sneer he demanded, "Give me my pouch."

"Here, take it," gasped Wayne. With trembling fingers he pulled it out and the pirate snatched it.

Tall John reached down and touched J.B.'s neck. "He's not dead, but he'll be out for a while. Or we could use him for fish bait if he dies!"

He grabbed J.B. and started dragging him face down through the sand. Wayne watched in horror as his friend remained as limp as a rag doll. One Eye put Wayne down on the sand. "Now, cabin boy, you can be smart or do you want to be stupid like your friend?" and he nodded toward Tall John dragging J.B.

Gathering his senses, Wayne replied, "Oh, I'll be very smart, sir.....very, very smart." He quietly started walking with the pirates. As they rounded a group of rocks, Wayne spotted a small boat pulled up on the sand. He winced. "How did we miss seeing this boat?" He looked to J.B. -- still unconscious. Tall John picked up the boy and threw him into the small boat. J.B. landed with a thud and moaned softly. Wayne rushed over to him, calling his name. "J.B., J.B., can you hear me? Please, please....answer me!"

One Eye grabbed Wayne and pushed him face first into the boat. "Oh, quit being an oyster...soft and mushy. Your friend is still breathing so he will live."

One Eye climbed in and Tall John pushed the boat off the sand. Jumping in, both pirates began rowing toward the big ship. Wayne watched nervously as they approached the vessel. He read the inscription on the side of the boat, *The Black Shark.* "Oh my goodness," he thought. He glanced at his watch. "It is 3:58. I'm not in the art room cleaning. I am about to board a pirate ship called *The Black Shark.*" Wayne shuddered at the very thought of what was waiting in store for him and J.B.

When they pulled alongside the ship Tall John yelled, "Ahoy, send down a rope. We've dead cargo to haul!" Looking at Wayne's stricken face he laughed. "Instead, make two ropes for two cabin boys!" He and One Eye started to laugh. Wayne looked at J.B., still unconscious. He looked at the two cruel pirates. He looked at the dark sides of the ship. He closed his eyes and took a deep breath. What would become of them?

CAPTIVE!
3

Wayne fidgeted as the rope was lowered from the *Black Shark.* Tall John roughly moved J.B., still unconscious, and wrapped the rope around his stomach. "There, that should hold him. Maybe if it breaks he'll fall in the water and wake up!" He laughed and looked sideways at Wayne. "Take 'er away!" He motioned and the rope tightened, lifting the freckle faced boy upward until the pirates pulled his body over the side of the ship.

Wayne sat nervously watching the rope's return. Suddenly One Eye grabbed the neck of his shirt. "You're next, Cabin Boy!" he sneered. Standing stock still, Wayne stood with his head down, defeated. Quickly One Eye wrapped the rope around his stomach. He yanked it, checking to see if it was secure, then used another piece to tie his hands. "O.K.," he yelled.

Wayne was jerked off his feet. He went limp, barely watching the boat as he was hauled upward. As he reached the top, another pirate grabbed him and shoved him onto the deck of the ship. Landing face first on the planks, he winced in pain. Rolling over because his hands were tied fast, he looked for J.B.

Seeing him tied to a pole, he breathed a sigh of relief. The pirate grabbed his neck and pushed him over to the post beside J.B. Wayne sat down.

One Eye walked over and instructed the other pirate. "Tie both these cabin boys together. Don't give them any food or water. When they work, they will eat!" and he turned away, laughing.

Wayne glared at him.

Suddenly One Eye spun around. Grabbing Wayne by the chin, he stared with his cruel black eyes. "Got a problem with this, Cabin Boy?" Wayne stared blankly at the pirate, saying nothing.

Pushing Wayne's head hard against the pole, One Eye grunted and stomped away.

Wayne sat quietly looking at the sky, glancing from time to time at his friend. "J.B, J.B, hey, buddy, can you hear me?" Wayne spoke softly, hoping to get a response. He nudged J.B. with his leg. Suddenly he groaned. Excited at any response, Wayne nudged him again. "J.B....please wake up! Can you hear me?"

"Ahhhhh"....J.B. groaned again. His eyelids started to flutter. Finally he opened his blue eyes wide and blinked, staring at Wayne. "Where am I....what happened?" he asked. "Oh, man, does my head hurt. What did I do? Hit a tree?"

Wayne replied, "Yeah, you hit your head on a tree alright! Do you remember playing on the beach and the time portal?"

J.B. answered, "Yeah....then I remember someone grabbing me. I remember biting some hairy arm." He paused and looked straight up in the air. "Oh, good grief! Are we on that pirate ship?"

"Yeah, I see you spotted the Jolly Roger flag," Wayne chimed in. "Brilliant discovery, Cabin Boy!"

J.B.'s eyes blazed with anger, "Oh, no...I'm not gonna be a cabin boy. I'm getting out of here!" he exclaimed.

"Now, J.B., just how are we gonna manage that?" Wayne asked. "Figure the facts. We're tied up, don't know where we are, and you've been injured."

J.B. replied, "I feel fine now. We need to get back to the beach, and I'm gonna free myself!" Wriggling his hand down his pant leg, he reached for his pocket. "Man these ropes hurt," he muttered. Turning slightly he bent his leg. He inched his hand into the pocket and fetched out the jackknife. "Grandpa always says a boy needs to be prepared!" He smiled, grasping the knife in his hand.

"What are you cabin boys up to?" a voice echoed across the deck.

J.B. and Wayne saw a pirate walking over to them. Quickly J.B. curled the knife back under his hand, hoping the pirate didn't see it.

"Well, well, well....our little cabin boy woke up." The pirate grabbed J.B. by his hair.

"Ouch... stop it!" J.B. winced in pain. Wayne quickly spoke, "Yes, we're both awake and ready to work." He smiled sweetly at the pirate, then turned and winked at J.B.

"Oh, yeah, I can work now. I'm fine. I won't run away," J.B. responded.

"Yeah, right. I'll tell Tall John," the pirate replied and scurried away.

"Whew, that was a close one," breathed J.B. He turned the knife over and opened the blade. Sliding it under the ropes, he freed both his hands.

Wayne nudged J.B.'s arm. "Listen, do you hear anything?" Noises came from below deck.

"Sounds like they're fighting...What time is it?" J.B. asked.

Wayne looked at J.B.'s watch. "It's 4:10."

J.B. shook his watch... "It's not broken, but how can it be 4:10 when the sun is close to setting?"

Wayne shook his head, looking puzzled, "Don't forget we came through a time portal. Time must be altered or something."

"We can't escape now in the daylight," J.B. spoke, looking around to make sure no one was on deck.

"Oh...do you mean we have to wait until dark?" queried Wayne. J.B. shook his head yes.

Minutes turned to hours as the boys sat on the hot deck of the ship. The sun sank below the horizon. Pirates walked by sneering and laughing at the boys. Wayne tried to make light of a hopeless situation and started to laugh.

"What's so funny?" J.B. asked.

"Oh, now I know what I never want to dress up like again! They're ugly and they smell bad!" Wayne mockingly closed one eye, mimicking the last pirate that walked by, "Arrrr.....cabin boy!"

J.B. laughed, "You're always good for a laugh, Wayne."

"Hey, how about some water!" yelled Wayne as a pirate walked by. A dim flicker of hope came to the boys' minds as they watched the pirate pick up a bucket near the stern of the ship, then strolled back to the boys.

"How's this, Cabin Boys?" growled the pirate as he dumped half rotten fish bait on their heads.

"Awww....get it off my head...awww...!" yelled Wayne in surprise. Sputtering and coughing, both boys shook their heads. J.B. started to pick up his hand but quickly remembered he was being watched. He dropped his head and continued to spit and cough. The pirate laughed and walked away.

"Oh, how I hate them!" exclaimed Wayne. "I hope a shark eats him!"

"Hey, it's not nice to hate anyone, even if they're mean," retorted J.B. "My mom says hate just grows like a nasty wound and gets worse."

"Then what are you supposed to do, give them a hug?" Wayne asked sarcastically.

"No, not exactly....I know it's hard to understand. I just know that inside I always feel better," answered J.B.

The darkness deepened on the deck. The ship rocked to and fro. Sea gulls flew overhead...their cries filling the air. For several minutes the boys were quiet, each lost in his own thoughts. The endless rocking continued. Both boys were getting very, very tired. Sleep soon overtook them and they both closed their eyes, free from all worries and cares.

Loud voices woke the boys from their sleep. The pirates tramped down the wooden steps below deck. A young boy appeared behind one of the pirates and slowly limped across the planks.

"Hey, Wayne, look! That pirate kid looks about our age," J.B. exclaimed. "Hey, you! Hey, kid! Come here!" J.B. yelled to the young man.

Startled, the boy tripped. Regaining his balance, he looked directly at the boys. He smiled and waved his arm.

"Toby, get going or I'll break your other leg!" A surly pirate grabbed the boy by his neck and kicked him.

"Awwwww...yes sir...yes sir!" Toby cried. Trembling with fear and pain, he looked away from the boys and quickly hobbled down the stairs.

"Did you see that? That was so mean!" J.B. tried to hold back tears. "That kid is like us. Why is he here?"

"Don't know, J.B., but we have to get ourselves out of here first, understand?" Wayne whispered.

The clatter of metal and the smell of food wafted to the boys on deck. "They must be eating. Good! Maybe they will go to sleep soon," said J.B., licking his parched lips.

"Boy, I'm sooo thirsty," grumbled Wayne. The voices below deck grew faint.

"Maybe they're drunk or something. I hope they passed out," muttered J.B. He reached down, cutting the ropes off his legs. Leaning over, he cut Wayne's ropes. The boys jumped up and looked over the side of the ship. "Wow, I can see the beach. I don't think we've moved. They must have anchored the ship, thank goodness!"

Suddenly they heard footsteps stomping up the stairs. The boys ran back to their spots, grabbed their ropes, and pretended to be asleep.

Tall John strolled over to see the boys. "Good, they're out like a light. We'll take them back ashore tomorrow and make them work." He chuckled and clumped away.

Cautiously the boys waited several minutes, then J.B. slowly opened his eyes.

"He's gone," he whispered.

Wayne opened his eyes. J.B. quietly jumped up and looked over the end of the ship. "How strong of a swimmer are you, Wayne?"

Wayne joined him and replied, "I can swim two lengths of the pool at the Y."

"Think you can go for four lengths?" J.B. wondered.

Wayne's face turned pale, "I don't know."

J.B. noticed the look of fear in Wayne's face and promised, "Hey, we can swim side by side. Just you and me, Buddy. We'll pretend we're at the Y, O.K?"

"O.K," Wayne bravely replied.

"Take off your shoes," J.B. instructed Wayne as he took off his own shoes. Within a minute he gripped Wayne's hand and they stood together on the railing, breathing deeply. "I'll count 1, 2, 3....then jump!" J.B. explained. "One, two, three..." and together both boys jumped into the dark water.

Still holding hands, J.B. pushed through darkness to the surface. Sputtering, he dog paddled. "Wayne, are you O.K.?"

"Yes, I'm O.K. You can let go of my hand. I'm not a baby!" Wayne spoke confidently.

"To the shore then!" cried J.B. Both boys started swimming toward the beach.

J. B.'s heart pumped with excitement as he took each stroke. Breathe, head under, breathe, head under. He kept a steady rhythm. The water felt good on his hot parched skin. Breathe, head under, breathe, head under.

Wayne tried not to think of how deep the water was. Pretend you're at the Y, pretend you're at the Y. He made a singsong of the thought.

The moon shone full on the glistening calm water, a beautiful sight to behold. The only irregular waves were the ones the boys were making. A dark fin crested to the right of the boys. The dark foreboding water held a terrible secret.

J.B., unaware of the lurking danger, kept thinking of his only goal...reach the shore. J.B.'s right leg kicked into the darkness and a horrible pain shot through his right leg. Hot fire and thousands of needles penetrating his skin jolted J.B. into fear mode. Something started dragging him down, deep into utter darkness. J.B. struggled and tried to kick with his left leg. His foot felt something squishy. In a split second he realized what was pulling and biting him! A shark! Panic overcame him and he continued kicking with his left leg, his right leg still held fast by the shark's jaws. "I'm gonna drown...I'll never see home again." The horrid truth became real. He thought of his family, his friends, his school, and his pets. "No, I'm not!" he thought. Power surged through him, giving him an adrenalin rush. Twisting his body around, he made a fist and hit with all his might into the soft squishy snout of the shark again and again. He was running out of air!

One last punch, the shark finally released his grip on J.B.'s leg. J.B. shot to the surface, gasping for air. Looking around for Wayne he yelled, "Help me, Wayne! Oh, please help me!"

"I'm here! We're almost there. What's the matter?" asked Wayne, completely oblivious to the shark attack.

"There's a shark. Watch out! He attacked me! He's coming back!" J.B. screamed.

The mention of the word shark was all Wayne needed to spring into action. Swimming close to J.B. he said, "Come on....you've got time. Easy does it. We're almost there." His words of comfort were all J.B. needed to refocus. Wayne nervously glanced over his shoulder, looking for the shark. There! He saw a dorsal fin coming from the right! Refusing to think the worst, he grabbed a hold of J.B., guiding him through the water to the shore.

When J.B.'s feet touched the sand, he winced in pain. Unable to stand, he crawled. Wayne reached down and helped J.B. half hop, half walk to the top of the beach. Blood gushed from the open wound on J.B.'s lower leg.

"Oh, good grief!" Wayne stopped and yanked his t-shirt off his back, quickly tying it around his friends leg. "We need to stop the blood flow! Here, hold this."

He placed J.B.'s hand on the t-shirt. "Now, where's the time portal?"

"Over there by the palm tree." J.B.'s words were barely audible. He started to point then dropped on the sand.

"You're going into shock!" cried Wayne. He dragged the weakened J.B. over to the palm tree and staggered into the time portal. The lights around the door were still blinking green.

Once inside the tunnel, Wayne fished out his flashlight, stuck it under his arm, and started dragging his friend away from the portal. "J.B., can you hear me?" He continued a dialogue as they hurried through the tunnel. J.B. moaned with each step. Wayne finally saw the glimmer of light coming from the art room. He cried, "We're here! We made it! Now let's find your grandfather!"

Laying J.B. gently on the floor of the art room, Wayne ran out the door. "Mr. Hritzay....Mr. Hritzay...help! J.B.'s hurt!" Frantically Wayne ran down the next hall.

Mr. Hritzay stepped out into the hall. "Hey what's all the yelling for? I can hear you loud and clear!"

"It's J.B. He's hurt! He's bleeding!" Wayne shouted.

"Bleeding, hurt, what happened? Never mind....where is he?" Mr. Hritzay started to run after Wayne down the hall. Arriving at the art room, Mr. Hritzay quickly picked up J.B. and ran down the hall. Wayne opened the side door and together they headed to his pickup. Placing J.B. in the front seat, Mr. Hritzay jumped into the truck and Wayne found a small space to sit.

"There's an old shirt behind the seat. Grab that and put it on," Mr. Hritzay told Wayne.

Roaring out of the parking lot, Mr. Hritzay looked at both boys. "I thought I told you two not to mess with the paper cutter! Why didn't you listen?" he looked sternly at both boys. "And why are you wet? Where are your shoes?"

"Gee, I'm sorry, Grandpa!" J.B. trembled in pain.

Wayne quipped, "Honestly, sir.....we didn't mean to cause harm!"

"Well, boys, harm is done...I want some answers when this is through!" Mr. Hritzay slammed on the brakes at the emergency room entrance. Running around the truck, he carefully picked up J.B.

4
TO TELL THE TRUTH

The hospital door opened. Mr. Hritzay carefully carried his grandson through the entrance. Wayne ran up beside them and pointed to the desk. "Quick! Over here!"

The nurse on duty looked up from the desk.

"Hurry! His leg is bleeding. Where do we go?" Mr. Hritzay asked in a trembling voice.

"Well, I need to have you sit..." the nurse started to say, then noticed the blood soaked t-shirt. "No, never mind. Come, follow me."

She briskly walked down the hall, Mr. Hritzay and Wayne following. Pushing back the curtains of an exam room, she turned to Mr. Hritzay and said, "Here, put him on this bed." While Mr. Hritzay gently lay J.B. down, she asked, "What happened?"

Mr. Hritzay spoke quickly, "The boys were cleaning for me. I told them not to mess with the paper cutter in the art room."

J.B. started to groan, moving his injured leg. Blood seeped from the t-shirt onto the clean white sheets. The boy's eyes opened and he tried to sit up.

"Just wait," the nurse ordered. She pulled back the curtain, revealing the long hallway and spoke, "Dr. Andric, we need you right now! Bleeding leg wound in exam 5."

Turning back, she gently pushed J.B. back on the pillow. "Just lie down, son, and rest." Patting his curly red head, she motioned to Mr. Hritzay and Wayne to sit down.

The curtain parted and a young, blond haired doctor entered the cubicle. "Hello, I'm Dr. Andric. Let's see this wound." He took some scissors and carefully started to cut away the blood soaked t-shirt. Sand sprinkled off the shirt and onto the floor. Brushing the sand away from the cut, Dr. Andric began cleaning away the dried blood.

"Ouch!" protested J.B.

Dr. Andric said, "I'm sorry, son, but this is going to hurt. Will you be okay?" He smiled and looked at the face filled with fear. J.B. grimaced in pain but slowly shook his head.

Skillfully probing the wound, Dr. Andric took tweezers and pulled several pieces of seaweed and mangled skin off the leg. Laying each piece in the small dish beside the bed, he looked puzzled. "Hey, what is your name?" he asked his patient.

"J.B.," came the reply. "Really my name is James Bud, but people call me J.B. I'm named after my great-grandfather."

"Well, J.B.," wondered Dr. Andric, "can you tell me what happened? Were you swimming?"

"Uh," he hesitated.

Wayne quickly jumped in, "Well, sir, we were playing by the paper cutter. I opened it and J.B. jokingly put his leg in it. My hand slipped and I dropped the cutter on his leg!" Wayne started to cry. "I'm sooooo sorry!"

J.B. moaned, "Hey, Wayne...it was an accident. I forgive you! Don't cry, please!"

The doctor looked baffled. "Boys," he asked slowly, "how large is that paper cutter?" He continued pulling out chunks of seaweed.

"Oh--um--about 2 feet. It's a big cutter," answered Wayne and J.B. nodded in agreement.

Dr. Andric pulled the pieces of jagged skin together, rinsed the wound thoroughly, then reached for the needle. He paused and turned toward J.B. "Well, young man, I'm going to give you a shot. It will just be a little pinch but it will be a great help to you. I have a lot of stitching to do. This way you won't feel anything." He winked at the boy. The nurse walked in and handed the doctor a syringe. Gently Dr. Andric pushed the needle into J.B.'s leg.

J.B. swallowed and grunted, "Hey, sir, that wasn't bad! Thank you."

Dr. Andric smiled as he threaded the needle into his leg. Expertly guiding the needle, he sewed the jagged skin together. J.B. closed his eyes. Mr. Hritzay and Wayne sat very quietly watching the whole procedure. Within minutes the doctor finished and he patted J.B.'s uninjured leg. "Hey, Buddy, you can open your eyes. I'm done." Dr. Andric smiled at the boy. "You acted like a trooper."

Turning to Mr. Hritzay and Wayne, the doctor continued, "Well, guys, we're out of the woods now." Then he folded his arms and gazed, perplexed, at both boys. "Now let's get down to business." Looking at Mr. Hritzay, Dr. Andric asked, "Sir, where did you say you found the boys?"

Mr. Hritzay seemed alarmed and answered, "I was cleaning down the hall. Wayne came running to tell me J.B. was hurt. I ran to the art room and found J.B. on the floor, bleeding!"

"In the art room?" Dr. Andric scratched his head.

"Yes, the art room," replied Mr. Hritzay.

The doctor frowned and looked back and forth between the two boys. "Boys, did you really play with the paper cutter or did you do something else?"

J.B. and Wayne both feigned innocence and answered in unison, "The paper cutter."

Dr. Andric sighed and shook his head as he paced by the bed. "I've seen this type of wound before. Before I came to this hospital I worked for a year in the Bahamas."

"Wow, sir," cried J.B., "did someone there have a paper cut injury, too?"

Dr. Andric shook his head. "No, it was something more serious--a shark bite!"

J.B. and Wayne's faces turned white and their jaws dropped open. Dr. Andric studied their facial expressions while Mr. Hritzay stared at the boys.

"So," continued Dr. Andric, "how did you happen to get bitten by a shark in the art room? Look at the sand on the floor and all the seaweed I pulled from the wound. Plus your clothes are all wet."

J.B. hung his head. "You'll never believe me--no one will believe us." Wayne shook his head in agreement. "But here goes...we got captured by pirates, had to jump ship and swim for the shore. I was attacked while I was swimming."

"Oh, for Pete's sake, J.B., tell the truth!" Mr. Hritzay pleaded.

"I am telling the truth, Grandpa! I really am! It all started with the hole in the wall." J.B.'s voice was firm and steady.

Wayne piped up and added, "There's this picture of a jaguar in the art room. J.B. saw its eyes blinking in art class. That's why we wanted to clean there. There's a hole behind the closet wall. Actually, it's a tunnel--a time portal! Do you believe in time portals? They really do exist!"

Dr. Andric appeared amused but continued to listen. "Can you show me this time portal?"

Mr. Hritzay spoke up, "Doctor, I'm the school custodian. I have access to the school any time. Would you like to take a trip there now?"

Dr. Andric smiled and shook his head. "Well, I can't right now because I'm on duty. But yes, let's make a date to see this time portal."

Mr. Hritzay wrote down his phone number on a piece of paper and then handed it to the doctor. "There is the number--call any time. Is there anything we need to do about this wound, Doctor?"

The doctor smiled and looked at J.B. "No, just keep it clean and no swimming! We'll have to remove the stitches in a week. Stop and make an appointment with the nurse before you go." He shook J.B.'s hand. "You're a brave boy and a good story teller." He winked at the boys.

"Dr. Andric, Dr. Andric, room 8, stat," blared the intercom. Dr. Andric pulled the curtain back and stepped into the hallway.

"Well, guys, I gotta go. Take care." He turned and quickly walked down the hall.

J.B. glanced at Wayne and whispered, "Whew--that was too close! I hope they don't believe us." He gazed over at his grandpa.

"Well, gentlemen, let's go. I think we all need some fresh air." Mr. Hritzay got up from his chair.

J.B. gingerly stood up from the bed. Putting his good leg forward, he attempted to walk. Wayne and his grandfather steadied him.

"Whoa, young man, where do you think you are going?" cried the nurse as she reentered the exam room.

"Oh, I'm sorry. I thought when the doctor left we were free to go," apologized Mr. Hritzay.

"Well, yes and no," explained the nurse. "I need you to sign these papers before he is released. You're his grandfather, right?"

"Yes, Ma'am," replied Mr. Hritzay, then sighed. "I just need to explain this to his mother."

After signing the papers, Mr. Hritzay handed them back to the nurse. "Is there anything else we need to do?"

Shaking her head, she smiled. "No. Return in one week to have the doctor take out the stitches. I hope the rest of your day is better. Stay away from pirates!" She laughed.

The boys laughed with her and nodded their heads. "You bet!"

Carefully maneuvering down the hall, J.B. asked, "Grandpa, are you ever gonna let us clean again?"

Grandpa chuckled. "Oh, I might, but I definitely want to see this time portal, though! Let's go home and talk to your mother. Then we'll go back to the school."

"Sounds like a great idea. I can hardly wait to show you," said J.B. He glanced at Wayne and winked.

Climbing into the truck, J.B. spoke. "Mom's gonna have a hissy fit when she sees me. I know I'll be grounded, Grandfather."

"Well, you should have thought of that before this whole episode started," chided Mr. Hritzay.

"Hey, maybe she'll want to see the time portal, too!" piped Wayne.

"Oh, great! We might as well sell tickets," moaned J.B. sarcastically. He slouched back in the seat and stared out the window.

Mr. Hritzay turned down Pearl Street and pulled into J.B.'s driveway.

"Hey, your mom's home," Wayne smiled and added, "Oh boy, now you're gonna get it!"

"Oh boy, now you're gonna get it!" parroted J.B., giving Wayne a dirty look.

"Boys, stop it. Just be glad you're O.K. and home," scolded Mr. Hritzay.

Climbing out of the truck, the three walked to the side door and knocked. Mr. Hritzay yelled, "Laurie, I brought J.B. home."

Mrs. McBride opened the door. "Oh, Dad, thanks so much." Looking down at her son's bandaged leg, she cried, "J.B., what on earth happened?"

"Aww, Mom, it's not too bad. Let me explain." He stood up straight, trying to look fine.

Mr. Hritzay spoke quickly and ushered the boys inside the house to sit down, "No, really, Laurie, let me explain. J.B. asked me after school if he could help clean the classrooms. I assigned Wayne and him to the art room. I'm afraid they were messing around and J.B. got cut with some type of sharp art tool."

"Mom, I'm sorry. I won't do it again, I promise," vowed J.B.

Wayne spoke up, "Mrs. McBride, I'm so sorry! I was the one who got the art tool out."

J.B.'s mom looked sadly at her son. "I promised your dad I would always watch out for you." She paused and took a deep breath. "How can I keep you safe when you do things like this?" She started to cry.

Mr. Hritzay gently hugged his daughter. "Laurie, you do the best you can. Max trusted you. He knew you'd take care of his son. I'm partly to blame because I let them clean unsupervised." He turned to look sternly at both boys.

"Oh, Mom...I'm sorry...I'm soooooo sorry," apologized J.B., hugging his mother.

Mrs. McBride gave her son and dad a hug. Then she reached to Wayne, pulling him into the hug. "O.K., guys, I guess we'd better thank the good Lord that everything is O.K. What did the doctor say, Dad?"

"Well, J.B. needs to report back to the hospital in a week to get the stitches out. No swimming. Just try to keep the wound clean and dry."

"Now, son, what happened exactly?" asked his mother.

"Here's the kicker, Laurie," explained his grandfather. "The boys told the doctor and me a wild story about a time portal in the wall in the art room. They said they were captured by pirates, had to jump off a ship and swim to shore, and then J.B. claimed he was attacked by a shark. The thing is, they were all wet and their shoes were gone."

"J.B., really? I thought you had given up telling tall tales. Don't you think that's a little bizarre? What did you do? Chop up your shoes and have a water fight?" Mrs. McBride looked her son in the eye.

J.B. Squirmed under her direct gaze and answered sheepishly, "Mom, I told the doctor I got cut by the paper cutter. He took a look at my wound and said it was a shark bite."

"Why would he think it was a shark bite?" questioned his mom.

Mr. Hritzay spoke up, "The doctor pulled seaweed from the wound and it was all over J.B.'s leg and clothes."

Mrs. McBride shook her head. "Now I'm totally confused."

"So am I," Mr. Hritzay nodded in agreement. "I don't get it."

Suddenly both Father and daughter looked at Wayne sitting quietly, looking out the window.

"Wayne, you're awfully quiet. Do you have anything to add to this mystery?" inquired Mrs. McBride.

"W-W-What?" Wayne stammered.

"I repeat, can you tell us in your own words what happened?"

Wayne gulped. "O.K., we got busted. We found a time portal, got captured by pirates, jumped ship, I mean the *Black Shark*, and swam. J.B. was attacked by the shark on the way to the beach." He finished with a sigh and shuddered.

"Oh, this is getting even better," Mrs. McBride said sarcastically. "O.K., boys, I want to see this time portal. Let's go." She turned to her father and asked, "Dad, can we go to the school now?"

"No, I'd rather wait until Dr. Andric can go with us--he's on duty right now. So we'll have to wait until he can come. Besides, I need to clean up the blood in the art room."

Mrs. McBride heaved a huge sigh. "Oh, all right. Did he say when he'd be available?

Mr. Hritzay shook his head. "No. I guess we'll have to wait."

"Come on, Wayne," prompted J.B. as he slowly rose from the couch.

"And just where do you think you're going, sir?" asked his mother.

"Mom, it's just to my room. Is that O.K.?"

Mom appeared to think about it for a minute. "Well, I guess you had a rough day. Yes, that's O.K. However, if Dr. Andric calls, then we are going to the school. Understand?"

"Got it, Mom," answered J.B. with a thumbs up, slowly limping down the hall.

5
TRUTH OR NOT?

Wayne caught up with J.B. in the hall. "What do you want to do?" he asked his friend.

Opening his bedroom door, J.B. walked inside and motioned Wayne to enter. He closed the door. "Let's sit down. My leg really hurts." Sitting on the bed, J.B. shook his head. Looking very seriously at Wayne, he decided, "We have to make a plan."

"Make a plan!" exclaimed Wayne. "You're busted, J.B. Now three people know about the time portal. There's no secret! We're done!"

"I know we have to be honest. This is just embarrassing!" retorted J.B.

A knock sounded on the bedroom door. Mr. Hritzay opened the door and said, "Boys, Dr. Andric just called. He's off his shift in an hour and he wants to go see the time portal with us. Your mom wants to go too and is waiting for you in the living room. I have keys to the school. Most importantly, you boys need to show us exactly where this time portal is, so find some shoes for both of you to wear."

The boys looked at each other, got up from the bed, rummaged in the closet for some old sneakers, and walked down to the living room. "Let's meet Dr. Andric in the yard," suggested Wayne.

"Great idea," agreed Mr. Hritzay. He nodded to his daughter.

"Dad, I've got a few things to do before he comes. Call me when he gets here," Mrs. McBride requested.

"Hey, let's play catch!" cried Wayne as they waited outside.

J.B. gave him a dirty look. "My leg hurts, you ninny. Play catch yourself!"

"J.B.," scolded his grandfather, "Wayne was just trying to be creative. He forgot about your leg."

"Aw-- sorry," he apologized.

About an hour later a car pulled into the driveway and Dr. Andric got out. "Hi, guys," he greeted them. Looking at J.B. he asked, "How is your leg, J.B.?"

"It hurts, sir, but I can manage it," he answered.

"Well, good," said Dr. Andric. "Now I want to see the time portal." He winked at Mr. Hritzay. "Are we ready to go?"

"Wait," said Mr. Hritzay, "I'll get my daughter." He stepped onto the porch calling, "Laurie, are you ready? The doctor is here."

"O.K., Dad," came the reply and Mrs. McBride walked out on the porch brushing her red hair back. "Hello, Dr. Andric, glad you could come. Well, let's go." She motioned to her minivan. "Come on, I'll drive."

"Sounds like a good plan." said Dr. Andric. They all climbed into the silver minivan.

J.B.'s mom drove two blocks to the school. "Which way, Dad?" she asked, pulling into the parking lot.

"Laurie, pull over there to the back door. I have a key for that," replied her father. Mrs. McBride pulled to the back door. Everyone piled out of the minivan. Mr. Hritzay walked to the door and slowly took his key out, unlocked the door and motioned for everyone to go in.

The boys walked slowly through the door, looking at each other.

Dr. Andric said cheerfully, "Fine, now where do we go to begin our adventures?" He smiled at both boys.

"Oh, brother," muttered J.B. under his breath. "Here goes nothing."

Wayne excitedly spoke, "O.K., everyone, to the tunnel. The art room is on the second floor." He spoke matter-of-factly.

"Well, upstairs, here we come," murmured J.B.'s mom. Together they walked up the stairs.

When they reached the top, J.B. said, "Now Wayne and I will explain the sequence of events."

Wayne pointed to the third door. He opened the door, stepped inside, and turned on the lights. Everyone filed in behind him and looked around.

"This is a nice room. It looks normal to me," noted the doctor.

"I agree," said Mrs. McBride. "Dad, what do you think?"

"I don't know," replied Mr. Hritzay as he rubbed his chin. "The boys asked to clean here. The rest is still a mystery to me."

Dr. Andric walked over to the paper cutter. "Hey, boys, this cutter is quite large-- about 24 inches long. The blade is new. I don't see any blood here."

"Oh, Dr. Andric, the only blood I found in this room was by the closet," replied Mr. Hritzay.

"Did you already clean it up?" asked Dr. Andric.

"Yes, sorry," replied Mr. Hritzay. "That's a school policy. Any blood has to be immediately cleaned up."

"That's all right," said Dr. Andric. "Just show me where you cleaned."

Mr. Hritzay walked over to the closet and pointed to the floor.

"Now, boys, tell us what happened from start to finish," ordered Mom.

"O.K.," said J.B., taking a deep breath. "I found holes in the jaguar's eyes. Watch this." He poked his fingers through the jaguar's eyes.

"Wonderful-- now the jaguar is blind," remarked Dr. Andric. "What next?"

J.B. pulled his fingers out of the picture. "Well, I started knocking on the walls after I opened the closet door......see?" J.B. opened the closet door and knocked on the back wall....thud...thud...thud...he moved his hand along the bare wall. Klunck....klunck.... "Listen!" he stopped. Turning toward the group he asked again, "Did you hear that?"

"Hear what?" wondered Dr. Andric.

"Hear it echoing?" asked J.B.

"Well, sort of," replied Dr. Andric.

"Now what?" wondered Mr. Hritzay.

"Watch this!" exclaimed Wayne and he pushed the wall. It didn't budge. J.B. joined him and together they pushed the wall... nothing! "Aw, come on, J.B., push harder!" yelled Wayne. They tried to push it again.

"Here, let me help," offered Dr. Andric and together all three of them pushed.....to no avail.

Mr. Hritzay shook his head, "Boys, stop...stop...I'm afraid you have told us a whopper of a story. Now fess up!"

"But, Grandpa," protested J.B., "we are telling the truth. There is a hole behind this wall!"

"Sir!" cried Wayne, "We're not lying. It's real! It's real!"

Mrs. McBride shook her head sadly. "No...no....give it up! Do you boys think we're going to buy your story? We're not dumb!" she scolded. "Admit it .....there is no hole....YOU MESSED AROUND IN THE ART ROOM and then came up with this story to cover it up. I know you, J.B. I can read you like a book." J.B.'s mom continued, "You've always been a good story teller, but this one has gone too far. Shame on you for wasting Dr. Andric's time."

She turned to Dr. Andric, "I'm so sorry for leading you on a wild goose chase, Doctor."

"No, Ma'am," answered Dr. Andric, "I always try to remember what it was like to be a kid with an active imagination. I was always dreaming up adventures myself." He grinned and winked at J.B. and Wayne. "Well, boys, I need to go, but if the pirates ever show up again, give me a call...O.K.?"

"O.K." answered both boys dropping their heads. "Thank you for everything, Dr. Andric," said J.B. "I'm sorry I wasted your time."

"Hey, boys, that's life! Enjoy being boys!" Dr. Andric smiled and turned toward the door.

"I'm O.K.," he told Mrs. McBride. "I'll jog over to your house to get my car. Take care and see you around."

Mr. Hritzay frowned at the boys, "This has gone too far. I'm afraid I won't have you two cleaning for a while." He turned off the lights and firmly said, "Problem is solved and case is closed. Let's go home."

CODE RED!

"Where did those stupid cabin boys go?" muttered One Eye, stalking across the deck of the *Black Shark*. "They were tied here and now nothing! Tall John won't be happy. Neither will the rest of the crew." He picked up the cut ropes.

"One Eye, where's the cabin boys?" One Eye dropped the ropes and saw Tall John standing over the pile of ropes.

"Well, this is all I've found," griped One Eye. "Cut ropes, no cabin boys. They must have jumped ship and swam to shore."

"In these shark infested waters???.....Boy are they stupid!" laughed Tall John. "They must be shark bait by now."

"No, I don't think so," disagreed One Eye. "Let's go look for them. I'll get the boat."

"Let's make it quick then. We need to pull up anchor today," replied Tall John.

One Eye lost no time getting the rowboat ready. Soon he and Tall John were heading back to shore.

Tall John scanned the beach with his spy glass. "No sight of them," he said disgustedly. As they neared shore Tall John spotted the blood spattered sand.

One Eye spoke, "Well, someone got hurt. Looks like a lot of blood. It will be easier to track." His eyes traced the trail as he and Tall John jumped out of the rowboat and dragged it up onto the beach. "The trail goes up this small hill."

One Eye and Tall John followed the tracks until they stopped abruptly near an old palm tree. "Hey, they're gone!" exclaimed One Eye.

"Yes, and they just seem to disappear!" agreed Tall John. He took a step forward and half of him disappeared!

"Tall John!" yelled One Eye. "Stop....stop.!"

"What the....son of a sea serpent!" yelled Tall John. Quickly stepping backward, Tall John's eyes opened wide with shock!

"Say, Tall John, ya looks like you just saw a monster. The other half of you is back, too!" exclaimed One Eye.

"What do you mean the other half....my body has always been together. It never left, you idiot!" retorted Tall John. Tall John shook his head in wonder. "Did you even see the tunnel?"

Now it was One Eye that had a blank look on his face. "What tunnel?" he asked.

"I took one step in the sunlight and the next step I was in a tunnel. Some green things were floating around me," stated Tall John.

"Hey!" cried One Eye. "That must be where the cabin boys ran to! Let's go after them!" he exclaimed.

"O.K.," decided Tall John, "follow me." He stepped ahead, disappearing into nothingness.

One Eye nervously watched Tall John disappear, gripped his sword, and stepped into thin air!

"Hey, Tall John....Tall John!" yelled One Eye, blinking his eyes, trying to see in the dimness.

"I'm here!" Tall John answered. There stood Tall John beside some green blinking lights. Tall John looked at One Eye and said, "I don't know what those things are, but follow me. This is a tunnel."

Both pirates stumbled ahead. "Oh, I wish I had me a torch," muttered Tall John.

"Aye me too!" agreed One Eye as he banged his head against a stone in the tunnel.

"Well, at least we can't get lost when we're going forward," said Tall John. "Keep one hand on the wall."

The pirates, more intrigued than frightened, continued staggering through the long tunnel. After a long time Tall John spied a two tiny pin points of light. "Aye! One Eye, look ahead. I see some light!"

Approaching the light, the 2 pirates had to crawl through a bigger hole. Tall John peered through the small holes. His steely eyes spotted not one, but many cabin boys and girls! Turning back to One Eye, Tall John said, "We hit the jackpot! There's about twenty or so cabin boys and girls!"

"Let's get 'em!" suggested One Eye.

Tall John felt the wall. His hand followed a seam to the tunnel floor. He pushed. Nothing moved. Dragging his hand along the seam he caught a small piece of fabric. Pulling it out of the seam, he gave the wall a shove. The door groaned open. Tall John walked through and stood behind the large art easel while he studied the activity in the room.

"Good morning class," beamed Ms. Plum as the now seated kindergartners directed their attention to the art teacher. The entire class was dressed in pirate costumes.

"My, I see all of you remembered to dress like pirates. That is our art theme for this week! Today we will be drawing and painting our very own pirate pictures!" She smiled at everyone. "You are all my Buccaneer Pirates! You are brave! You are bold! You are fearless!"

"Now, let's start talking about what a pirate looks like," continued Ms. Plum. She turned to the small easel in front of her.

Drawing a circle, she started to make the head, body, and clothes of the pirate.

Tall John stepped from behind the large easel, his eyes fixed on the kindergarten class. Ms. Plum remained oblivious to Tall John's presence and concentrated on the drawing. A hush settled over the room. "Oh, good," she thought, "they're watching and listening today." Turning to the students, she saw their eyes spellbound on her drawing, or so she thought. "Oh, class, you are very attentive today. That's great!" One small blonde girl raised her hand.

"Not now, Tehya," said Ms. Plum. "I'll answer questions when the drawing is finished." She returned to the drawing, adding texture to the clothes. "Pirates," she said, "sometimes have mismatched clothes ... .because they're often on ships for long periods of time."

Tall John glared at the now frightened kindergartners. Ms. Plum continued, adding a patch on the pirate's face, covering one eye. Turning to the kindergarteners, Ms. Plum was delighted to see their eyes wide open in wonder and amazement.

Blond haired Tehya was waving her hand and wriggling in her seat. "Tehya, I just told you I'll answer questions when I'm finished." Ms. Plum turned to add the finishing touches.

Tall John nodded for One Eye to step inside the art room.

"Ms. Plum....Ms. Plum!" Tehya was frantically waving her hand. "Oh, Ms. Plum!" Ms. Plum turned around, frowning. Looking directly into Tehya's blue eyes, she said, "Tehya, I'm ALMOST finished. You are being very impatient. Unless you have something life changing.....I suggest you wait until I'm DONE!"

Tall John moved over, his hand gripping his sword. One Eye stood beside him.

"Ms. Plum," spoke Tehya very calmly, "your pirates look great. They look just like those two pirates standing over there." She pointed to Tall John and One Eye.

"What pirates?" wondered Ms. Plum. Tehya and the entire class pointed to Tall John and One Eye standing beside the large art easel.

Ms. Plum's face turned snow white. "Pirates!" she muttered and collapsed in a heap on the floor!

"Pirates!" screeched twenty frightened kindergarteners. Tall John and One Eye quickly grabbed at the closest children sitting there.

"No!" yelled Tehya, grabbing a paint brush from the table. "They're strangers! Run!" Running straight at Tall John, she used the brush as a stick poking at him. "Run,

Sally, run!" she shouted to the tiny little girl sitting frozen with fear. Suddenly the whole classroom erupted into a bedlam of screaming children rushing for the door.

A brave boy, Eric, held the door, pushing children out into the hall. "Run, run!" he yelled.

Trying to slow the pirates down, Tehya started grabbing paint brushes, paint cans, and water cans off the tables. "Help me!" she yelled to her classmates. Flinging art supplies at the pirates, several kindergarteners joined her, peppering the pirates with paint. As the last kindergartners ran through the door, Tehya moved closer to the exit. Tall John grabbed Tehya's arm. His feet slid on wet paint and he crashed to the floor. Tehya yanked herself free and ran out the door. Eric followed on her heels.

At the opposite end of the hall J.B. and Wayne were sitting in Mr. Greene's 4th grade class. The sound of noisy children drifted down the hall. Mr. Greene looked up from his desk. "J.B., would you mind closing the door? It seems the kindergarteners still don't know the meaning of quiet."

"Yes, sir," answered J.B. He limped slightly to the door and looked out. He saw the entire kindergarten class running down the hall. "Oh, brother," he thought, but his jaw dropped when he saw a pirate looking out the art room door! He slammed the door and leaned against it, breathing hard.

"J.B., was that necessary?" asked Mr. Greene.

J.B. gulped. "No, sir. Sorry, sir."

J.B. looked at Wayne and mouthed the words "pirates." Wayne nodded. The sound of frantic children was right outside the door.

Wayne stood up, walking to the door. "Mr. Greene," he said quietly, "I gotta go!" Before Mr. Greene could reply, Wayne and J.B. ran out the door.

J.B. stopped the last two kindergarteners. Recognizing Tehya, his next door neighbor, J.B. said, "Tehya, what happened?"

"Pirates came out from the wall!" she yelled. "There they are!" she pointed to the art room.

J.B. thought quickly. "Run to the office. Tell them code red! Run, Tehya...run!" and J.B. turned toward the pirate now racing toward him!

Wayne yelled as the pirate came barreling down the hall, "Watch out, J.B.! It's One Eye!"

One Eye didn't slow down; instead he ran right into J.B., knocking him to the floor. Hitting the ground. J.B. moaned "Oh, no, my leg!" Wayne helped him up and together they watched One Eye run down the stairs after Tehya!

Tehya and her class ran to the bottom of the stairs. Frightened and yelling, the kindergarteners ran past the office and through the front doors of the school. Remembering J.B.'s words, Tehya quickly darted through the office door. "Mrs. Miller....Mrs. Miller...help us....strangers.... pirates...code red!" yelled the brave little girl.

"My, you kindergarteners are very noisy today," scolded Mrs. Miller. But taking a look at Tehya's frightened face, she quickly asked, "What did you say?"

"I said there are pirates chasing us....we're scared!" Tehya's brilliant blue eyes and tear-stained face revealed the dangerous situation.

"Pirates? Oh, did the pretend pirates scare you?" inquired Mrs. Miller.

"No, real ones! Like him!" Tehya frantically pointed to One Eye running down the stairs.

Spying the blond girl, One Eye ran to the office door and tried to yank it open.

"Oh, no you don't!" she yelled, gripping the door knob with all her strength. One Eye yanked once more and she lost her hold on the door. Tehya fell to the floor. One Eye reached down and grabbed her hair. "Ow!" she hollered and sunk her teeth into One Eye's arm. One Eye shook his arm violently and she rolled across the floor. One Eye growled at Tehya and ran out the office door, continuing his pursuit of the other kids.

"Oh, Honey, are you O.K.? You were so brave!" cried Mrs. Miller as she helped Tehya to her feet. "Oh, the warning she yelled!" She punched in the number for all school access. "Code red! Code red!" Mrs. Miller called over the intercom. "Oh, I need to alert the principal and police!" she realized. Gripping the office phone, she dialed 911 and then the principal.

Ms. Burns ran into the office. "Mrs. Miller, where is my kindergarten class? They were supposed to be in art but the room's a mess and I found Ms. Plum on the floor. She said she fainted and the only words that come out of her mouth are....'pirates...pirates!' And, Tehya, why are you here? Where is the rest of the class?"

"Oh, Ms. Burns...they ran outside. The pirates are chasing them! Look!" explained Tehya as she pointed to nineteen kindergarteners running through the yard.

"Oh, my goodness!" exclaimed Ms. Burns. "Help, help!" She flew out the office door.

J.B. and Wayne came galloping down the stairs. Looking at Tehya and Mrs. Miller, they both zoomed through the front door with Tall John chasing after them!

7
FOWL PLAY

"Children, stop! I'll help you!" yelled Ms. Burns as she sprinted across the school yard.

J.B. and Wayne took off toward One Eye who was running near the playground. The screaming children and blaring sirens added to the chaotic scene. Several police cars pulled into the parking lot. Ms. Burns, Mrs. Miller, and two police officers were able to safely corral all the kindergarteners.

One Eye and Tall John, frightened by the cars, sounds, and lights, ran toward the woods. J.B. and Wayne followed them until they heard a police megaphone ordering them to stop. Knowing they were already in trouble, they both ran back to the school. Police cruisers sped down the side road after the two pirates.

J.B. and Wayne followed the kindergarteners inside. The halls were filled with students and teachers asking questions and cheering Teyha and her classmates.

A news reporter ran over to J.B. and Wayne. Pushing the microphone into their faces, he excitedly asked, "Where did those pirates come from? Isn't this week a pirate theme here? What happened?"

J.B., frozen with fear, shook his head and answered, "I saw them chasing the kindergarteners. I tried to help!"

Wayne, recovering his wits, grabbed the microphone and said, "They must have snuck into the school somewhere! I hope they never come back!" He patted his friend on the back. "This guy tried to save the day."

"Yeah, right, Bro.," J.B. sarcastically answered.

The news reporter moved on down the hall, questioning many students. The boys tried to blend into the crowd, unnoticed.

The school intercom blared with instructions for everyone to return to their regular classes. Reluctantly, the students started back to their rooms, still buzzing over the day's excitement.

Meanwhile, Tall John and One Eye crouched behind a stone as they paused to get their bearings.

"Where to, Tall John?" panted One Eye.

"Quick, follow me!" whispered Tall John. He ran down a muddy trail toward the tall trees. Both pirates gripped their swords as they ran through unfamiliar terrain.

Thirty minutes passed and they were now deep in the woods. Leaning against a tree, Tall John shook his head. "We need to get back to the ship. I have no idea where we are or what those strange things were that we saw today."

"Aye, ain't that the truth," agreed One Eye. "Shouldn't we go back to that building we ran out of?"

"Yeah, but those black and white wailing monsters will get us if we return there," muttered Tall John. "Well, let's try to retrace our steps." He walked in the direction they had come from.

"Say, Tall John, look! There's an opening through the trees! I see land and some buildings!" exclaimed One Eye after they had walked a few minutes.

Both pirates crept out of the trees and followed a white fence until they came to a small white building. No one else seemed to be around.

"Let's rest in here until it gets dark," suggested Tall John. He opened the door slowly, disturbing a few chickens. Flapping their wings, the chickens squawked and darted about, scattering feathers everywhere.

"Ah, hush up, you big dummies!" ordered One Eye.

He and Tall John shut the door. Finding a spot beside a roll of hay, Tall John sat down.

"One Eye, make yourself a comfy spot to rest." Tall John leaned back against the chicken coop door and closed his eyes. Feathers lined the top of his pirate hat.

One Eye settled in the opposite corner of the coop, peering out the little chicken door. Looking at Tall John with the feathers on his hat, he laughed. "Tall John, You're just one big chicken all right!"

"Alex, Brendon, it's time for you to feed the chickens!" Mrs. Byler smiled as she gave her two younger boys the new bag of chicken feed. "Remember to shut the gate when you're done and be careful not to break any eggs." She looked at her youngest son, Brendon. "Brendon, you need to listen to Alex. He will help you because this is your first time helping him." She smiled again and straightened her white cap.

The two little Amish boys walked down the sidewalk to the chicken house. Brendon was the first to reach the chicken coop door. He pushed the door. It wouldn't budge. He turned to Alex.

"Here, Brendon, I'll get it." Alex pushed hard a few times.

The chicken door vibrating awakened Tall John from his nap. Grunting in surprise, he suddenly realized where he was. He heard voices outside. "Hey, One Eye!" he croaked softly, "We've got company."

One Eye quickly pushed his back against the wall, hoping to blend in with the coop.

Outside Brendon became impatient, got down on all fours, and crawled up the chicken ladder. Peering inside the chicken coop, he saw the two men inside. Puzzled by their strange clothing, he quickly pulled his head out and rolled down the chicken ladder.

Alex tried pushing the door again and noticed Brendon rolling down the ladder. "Brendon, go ahead and crawl in the chicken coop. I can't get the door open." Alex nodded for Brendon to go inside.

"Funny men chickens," Brendon said, pointing to the chicken coop.

"No, Brendon, these are girl chickens. We call them hens, not men," Alex tried to correct Brendon.

Brendon smiled. "They're big men," he insisted.

Alex, not wanting to argue with his little brother, agreed. "Yep, big chicken men. Now crawl in like a good boy and get the eggs." Alex pushed Brendon up the chicken ladder and through the chicken door.

Tall John and One Eye sat very still, staring at the little Amish boy. Brendon smiled and started picking up eggs. "Oops!" exclaimed Brendon as he dropped an egg near

Tall John. Famished, Tall John quickly picked up the egg, stuffing it in his mouth. Brendon smiled. Looking at One Eye, he purposely dropped another on the floor near the pirate's feet. One Eye scooped it up and ate it. Brendon laughed and continued to go back and forth between the men, dropping eggs on the floor.

Alex heard Brendon laughing and the soft thud of eggs hitting the floor. "Brendon, stop it! I'm gonna tell Mom you're dropping them on purpose!" he shouted. "Get out here right now with all the eggs you have!" Alex heard Brendon mumble goodbye.

Brendon appeared at the chicken door. "The men chicken look funny," he giggled and crawled down the ladder.

Alex groaned and shook his head. "They're not men chickens. You have only two eggs?"

Brendon shook his head. "The men chickens ate them. I gave them some." Brendon smiled.

"Wait until we get in the house and I tell Mom!" warned Alex. "She won't be happy." He grabbed the egg basket and ran to the house.

"Mom, Brendon broke the eggs. I think he broke them on purpose!" Alex told his mother.

Mrs. Byler looked at Brendon standing by the door. "Brendon, I told you to be careful, remember? I want you to do big boy chores. Don't you want to do big boy chores?"

Brendon dropped his head. "Mom, I helped feed the men chickens."

Mrs. Byler looked at Alex, "And what are these men chickens?"

Alex shuffled his feet. "Oh, I don't know, Mom. I think he gets mixed up with the word hen and men. I heard him dropping eggs on the ground inside the coop."

"Weren't you with him in the coop, Alex? I told you to help him," scolded Mrs. Byler.

"Mom, the door was stuck, so Brendon climbed up the chicken ladder to get in," explained Alex.

"Oh, I see. One of your brothers will have to take a look at the door when they get home." Mrs. Byler turned toward the cook stove. "Well, I need to get these cookies out of the oven." She set the warm cookies on the table to cool. "Here, boys, you can each have two cookies. Now go and play until I call you for dinner."

The boys grabbed two cookies each. "Thanks, Mom!" they cried in unison and ran out the door.

A red truck pulled into the driveway. Alex poked his head inside the kitchen and hollered, "Mom, the neighbor just pulled in!"

Mrs. Byler wiped her hands on her apron and walked onto the side porch. "Oh, hi,

Cheryl. What's happening today? Where's Cody? In school?"

A tall blond haired woman got out of the truck. "Well, that's exactly what I want to tell you, Betty." She looked over to where the boys were playing. "I just got a call from Cody's school. Apparently there were two men dressed like pirates that got into the school today. They scared the kids and escaped. The police are looking for them. They could be anywhere, so you'd better keep the boys in sight so they're safe."

"Oh, thanks for telling me. David and the other boys are at the shop. I'm here myself with the two youngest till they get home. What do these men look like?"

"I guess they're dressed like pirates in mismatched clothes. They both had swords and one wore an eye patch," answered Cheryl. "Call me if you see anything weird. I'm just down the road. Don't forget, we neighbors watch out for each other!" Cheryl smiled and jumped back into the truck. Waving at Betty and the boys, she backed out of the driveway.

Alex and Brendon ran over to their mom. "Mom, what's wrong?"

Mrs. Byler frowned. "There was a scare at Cody's school today. Some men dressed like pirates tried to scare the children. The police are still looking for them. You're coming inside to play until your dad comes home."

Together they walked to the house. "Let's look at your new library books. That will give us something to do," decided Mrs. Byler. She took both boys by the hand and entered the living room.

Back in the coop Tall John and One Eye looked at the chickens.

"I'm tired of being cooped up like a chicken," complained One Eye. Standing up, he bumped his head on the rafters. "Ouch I know it's not dark, but I've got to get out of here!

"Aye," agreed Tall John. "I'm hungry and thirsty. That egg wasn't enough." Pushing the chicken door open, both sneaked out into the yard. The sun was beginning to set in the west.

"Good! It's almost time to get back to that building. First, let's find some water," suggested One Eye. He scanned the yard and sniffed. "Hey, I smell food!" He looked toward the house. "Come on, Tall John, food awaits!"

The pirates crept to the side porch. Cautiously they slunked up the steps. pushed the door open, and stepped into the kitchen. The tantalizing smell of fresh cookies permeated the room. The pirates walked over to the table and began to devour the cookies.

In the living room, Mrs. Byler asked her sons, "Show me your favorite book."

Brendon quickly gave her the book on ships. Sitting down on the couch together, he turned the pages.

"Whoa, not so fast!" laughed Mrs. Byler as she looked at the various ships. Alex walked over to the couch and sat beside them.

Brendon turned the pages until he stopped at the pirate ship.

"Wow, Brendon, is that your favorite ship?" Mrs. Byler asked her son.

Brendon smiled and pointed to the pirate with the parrot on his shoulder. "Chicken men," he stated, smiling. "Funny chicken men."

"Oh, not again," muttered Alex. "Mom, he needs to get straight about chickens."

"Now, wait a minute, Alex," murmured Mrs. Byler, "we're not looking at chickens. We are looking at--pirates?" She stopped suddenly. Studying the picture, she asked Brendon, "Brendon, have you seen chicken men before? Did you see any chicken men today?"

Brendon nodded and laughed. "Funny chicken men like to eat eggs."

Mrs. Byler's face paled. "Boys, stay here and look at the book. I will go get us some more cookies." She stood up and quickly walked to the kitchen.

"Oh my goodness!" she gasped as she turned on the kitchen light. Two surprised pirates with cookie crumbs on their faces stood near the kitchen table!

Tall John reached for his sword. Mrs. Byler grabbed her rolling pin. More angry than frightened, she yelled, "Get out! Get out!" Protecting her children gave her the courage of a wild tiger and she ran toward the pirates, swinging the rolling pin like a banshee. She hit One Eye on the head. He screamed in pain and ran for the door.

"Go, Mom, go!" cheered Alex and Brendon as they watched the excitement unfold.

Looking back at her children, she hollered, "Boys, get back! Get back!" She lunged at Tall John. Tall John avoided the rolling pin by jumping sideways. One more jump and he ran out the door behind One Eye. Mrs. Byler chased the pirates across the yard. "Get out of here!" she screamed.

The pirates lost no time sprinting out of the yard. They ran down the road and disappeared from sight.

Mrs. Byler stood in the yard. Holding her rolling pin above her head, a smile appeared on her face. Alex and Brendon ran out to her.

"Wow, Mom! You were so brave! I wish Dad could have seen you in action!" Alex and Brendon danced around their mom in a victory dance.

Mrs. Byler smiled at her two young sons. "Yes, just wait until David and the older boys get home. They'll never believe our adventures!"

8
ON THE RUN

One Eye and Tall John raced down the road, away from the screaming Amish mother, away from the screaming children, away from the squawking chickens.

Looking side to side along the dirt road, Tall John spotted some bushes. "Quick! Over here!" he called to One Eye. They jumped behind the bushes to catch their breath. "Boy, you took quite a hit from that wild woman," Tall John noted. "Your only good eye is turning black and blue."

"Yeah, black and blue. It doesn't feel too good." He shook his head in disbelief. "I've never been attacked by a woman before. Tall John, don't tell anyone a woman hit me. I'll never hear the end of it!" One Eye ruefully rubbed his head.

"Well, we've got bigger problems than a wild woman," muttered Tall John. "We've got to get back to that building, find the tunnel, and get back on board the *Black Shark*."

"Aye, the *Black Shark* and the ocean," agreed One Eye.

"Careful then, let's walk along this dirt road. If we see anyone coming along, we'll hide," decided Tall John as he slipped out and continued walking down the road.

A while later the sun set and soon it was pitch black.

"Say, Tall John," exclaimed One Eye, "we'll be able to get around much better now. No one will see us. Hope you know where the building is."

"Don't know, but I'll find it," vowed Tall John.

The sky seemed to become lighter as they walked down the road.

"Aye, these people must have many torches," surmised One Eye.

"Torches or not, we need to get back to that large building." Tall John frowned. "We must not attract any more attention."

The road suddenly turned into a paved street with buildings on both sides. The pirates once again became very cautious, looking for any movement.

"Nothing! Let's walk between those two buildings." Tall John pointed to his left. Sliding into the shadows, the pirates paused. "Listen, do you hear anything?" Tall John asked One Eye.

"Nary a thing, mate," replied One Eye. He started walking a little faster, passing building after building, keeping to the shadows.

"We've been walking for quite a while. Remember the large grassy area we ran into from the building?" Tall John asked.

"Aye, the grassy area where we lost all the cabin boys?" answered One Eye.

"Yes, the grassy area. I don't see anything of the likes here." Tall John's voice sounded annoyed.

Minutes turned into hours as the pirates walked down the streets, hiding whenever vehicles approached with their eerie beams. The night lights obscured the stars, so the pirates kept going around in circles. The eastern sky became lighter. Dawn was approaching.

"We'd better find a place to hide. Soon there will be people about. I'm sure they're still looking for the likes of us!" warned Tall John.

"How are we gonna hide among these buildings? What about a house or something?" One Eye wondered.

Tall John laughed. "Don't tell me you want to hide in another chicken house? Or do you want to find another wild woman to knock some sense into your head?"

"Shiver me spine and head, no!" roared One Eye.

"Hey, look!" said Tall John, pointing to a sign lighted by a lamp--The Laughing Dolphin--Rest and Retirement Home. He turned to One Eye. "Looks like a resting place. There are little cabins. Let's see if any are empty."

They crept through the gate and Tall John opened the closest cabin door. Spying someone sleeping on a small cot, he quietly closed the door.

"How about this one?" whispered One Eye, opening the second cabin door. It appeared to be empty. "Quick, Tall John, in here!" One Eye motioned to the other pirate.

Closing the cabin door and bolting it, both pirates sat down on the two cots in the room.

"What is that white thing fastened on the wall?" asked One Eye.

Tall John shook his head. "Don't know. Never saw such a thing." He walked over to the white thing on the wall. Touching the silver fixtures close to the wall, he turned one. Water came splashing out. "Great fishhooks!" he yelled. He jumped back, watching the water continue to pour from the silver fixture.

"Hey, Tall John, it's water! Like it's straight from the ocean!" One Eye exclaimed.

"Hey, I don't want the whole ocean in here," worried Tall John, and he stepped forward to turn the silver fixture back. The water stopped flowing and Tall John squinted at the mirror above the white sink.

"Why look, I still have paint on my face since the run in with the cabin boys in that tunnel building." He tried to wipe the dried paint off his face. "Aye, it's all over our clothes, too, One Eye."

"I'd better get it off my clothes. It might make us look suspicious." One Eye took water from the sink and wiped it on his dirty clothes.

Tall John laughed. "Once a pirate, always a pirate! What you say we get some shut-eye?"

Wearily the two men collapsed on the cots and were soon snoring blissfully.

Tap, tap, tap. The door rattled and a voice called out, "Mr. Cox, Mr. Cox, are you coming out this morning to hear the children sing?"

Confused, Tall John bolted up on the cot, startled, and answered, "Uh--Yes, I'll be out, mate!"

"Well, Mr. Cox, I'm the new cabin helper. Please open the door so I can see you're all right. Did you have fun going to visit your family? Is that why you got back so late last night?"

Tall John, hoping to fit in and not raise an alarm, slid the bolt back and opened the door. A red headed teenage girl smiled as Tall John stood in the doorway.

"Hey, I like your pirate outfit. Is that a new look for the elderly? Who is the other elder with you? Your brother?"

The teen bubbled with more questions while Tall John wondered how he should answer. He finally cut in with, "Yeah, I got here late. This is my brother, One Eye. He's shy; he don't talk much." Tall John glared at One Eye, hoping he got the hint to remain quiet. "And yeah, these are my old clothes from the *Black Shark*, I mean home," Tall John stammered, hoping his slip wasn't noticed.

The girl shrugged. "Well, gentlemen, the children will be here to sing soon. Find a seat and make yourselves comfortable out there in the garden spot." The teen waved good-bye and walked toward the next cabin.

"Fish spit! That was too close," muttered Tall John as he closed the cabin door. "One Eye, we'll have to blend in with these people today and then get away to find that big brick building."

One Eye glanced out the cabin window. "Then let's go. It's a great day for pirates!" He slapped Tall John on the back, opened the cabin door, and sauntered over to the garden that sat in the middle of the cabins. Tall John followed close behind.

Looking around, Tall John sized up the other residents. "O.K., we'll fit in with these folks. Then we'll plan to leave at nightfall."

Children's happy voices echoed across the lawn. Tall John and One Eye saw children approaching. "Quick! Grab a seat!" ordered Tall John as the group came closer. There weren't many seats left.

One Eye sat down in the second row behind an elderly couple. Tall John joined him.

"Oh no," moaned One Eye.

"What now?" whispered Tall John.

"That's the group of cabin boys and girls we chased at the big building yesterday," replied One Eye.

"Shark bait!" spat Tall John. "And there's that yellow-haired girl who threw the paint at us."

Tall John and One Eye slid down in their lawn chairs, hoping the children wouldn't recognize them.

A woman stood in front of the audience. "Greetings, residents of the Laughing Dolphin. My name is Ms. Burns. I'm here with my kindergarten students to entertain you today. We will start by singing our sea chanty song. We learned these songs when we studied about pirates and the sea." She blew her pitch pipe and the students started to sing.

As they sang the kindergarten students looked at the group of elderly residents seated on the lawn. Excited to be outside, they waved to the people. Tehya stood in the front row. Glancing around, she spotted two elders in the second row, their heads down. She studied their clothing. The old man in front of the two moved his chair slightly, giving Tehya a better view. Tehya gasped. One had an eye patch and the other had blue paint on his pirate hat!

Nudging Eric, who stood beside her, she whispered, "Eric, look in the second row!"

Eric glanced at Tehya, then the audience. His eyes widened and he whispered back, "Oh no! It's them!"

Directing the group, Ms. Burns noticed the two students talking. She nodded her head and frowned at them. Tehya and Eric quickly regained their composure and finished the sea chanty.

While the concert continued, Tehya kept her eyes on the two intruders. Tall John and One Eye kept their heads bent and tried to melt into the chairs.

"One Eye, that feisty yellow-haired cabin girl is watching us. I think she recognizes us," Tall John spoke, his voice low and barely audible.

The kindergarteners continued their singing until Ms. Burns announced their last song. "Thank you for your attention and your hospitality. The class will end with the 'Pirate's Good-bye', a farewell song."

The students sang the song with gusto. Tehya and Eric riveted their eyes on the two pirates in the second row.

After the song faded, Ms. Burns stood near the path where the kindergarteners filed by to leave the garden. As Tehya walked by Ms. Burns, she stumbled. Ms. Burns caught her and gently asked, "Tehya, are you O.K.? You seemed preoccupied during the concert."

Tehya scowled and pointed to the second row. "Ms. Burns, it's the pirates!

Startled, Ms. Burns tried to quiet Tehya. "Tehya, dear, not now. We'll talk about this on the bus." Ms. Burns smiled and patted Tehya on the head.

Tehya straightened up and walked past the rows of people. Staring at Tall John and One Eye, her bright blue eyes never wavered. Tall John lowered his eyes, looking at the ground. One Eye sat frozen in fear. She turned and followed her classmates.

Stopping by the bus, Ms. Burns turned and asked, "Tehya, what pirates?"

"Ms. Burns, the ones that chased us yesterday! They were sitting there! Look! They're running away!" Tehya pointed to Tall John and One Eye running across the lawn.

"Oh, my goodness! Call 911!" cried Ms. Burns.

ALWAYS BE READY

Ms. Burns and her students quickly boarded the bus. Two police cars arrived and escorted them back to the school. As the children got off the bus, they were ushered directly into the building. Ms. Burns thanked the officers and followed her students. Stopping by the office, she told the principal about their brush with the pirates. He confirmed the school was beginning a lock-down mode.

In the hallway Tehya and Eric were in deep conversation about the pirates.

"I spotted them as soon as that one man moved his chair!" exclaimed Tehya.

"Yeah, they stood out like a sore thumb!" added Eric.

"I wonder where they're at right now," murmured Tehya.

"Class," Ms. Burns spoke with authority, "you all did very well singing today. Tehya, I'm so very sorry I didn't believe you when you first mentioned pirates. Please forgive me."

Tehya gave Ms. Burns a hug. "Oh, Ms. Burns, that's O.K. I understand."

An announcement came over the loudspeaker. "Teachers, the school is having a lock-down. Please see that all your students are in the classroom. Stay alert until further notice."

Walking back to their classroom, Tehya saw J.B. and Wayne hurrying down the hall. "J.B." Tehya waved her arms to stop him.

J.B. stopped, looking concerned. "Hey, Tehya, what's up? We're having a lock-down. Hurry, I gotta go."

"J.B., our class just saw the pirates. We were singing at the Laughing Dolphin and they were hiding in the audience!"

"Oh, my goodness!" exclaimed J.B. "Did you see both of them?"

"Yeah, both. They sat until the end of the program. Then they ran off!"

"J.B. and Wayne, get to your classroom, please!" Ms. Burns ordered, her voice filled with concern.

"Yes, Ms. Burns, we'll go. Thanks, Tehya," replied J.B. He and Wayne quickly walked down the hall.

Going up the stairs to their classroom, J.B. looked at Wayne and said, "Now we'd better think up a plan to get these pirates back to their time zone."

"Oh, yeah, and we're just gonna stop and ask them if they want to go home," Wayne added sarcastically.

"Not exactly, but you know what I mean," retorted J.B. as they walked into their classroom.

"Gentlemen, please close the door. We are in a lock-down," ordered Mr. Greene. "Class, open up your math books. Try not to worry about the lock-down. Let's start by playing a math game." Mr. Greene continued with his rules for the game.

J.B.'s mind was far away, trying to figure out creative ways to find the pirates and return them to their place in time. "Well, I'll just have to hang around school after dismissal. I bet those pirates are trying to find this place. Maybe they have put two and two together."

"J.B., it's your turn." Mr. Geene's voice surprised J.B. and he jumped. "J.B., are you okay?" Mr. Greene asked.

"Oh, I'm fine, Sir," replied J.B., then randomly picked a number.

"Not correct, sorry." Mr. Greene turned to Wayne. "O.K., you're next."

Wayne replied, "Fifty-eight is the answer."

"Right! Good job," praised Mr. Greene. The class continued playing the game. The last bell rang for the day.

A message blared over the intercom. "The lock-down is lifted. School is dismissed for the day. Please be advised to go straight home and report to your parents. There are still two intruders loose in town dressed as pirates."

J.B. walked down the hall to the custodian's room. "Grandpa! Are you here?" He left the room and walked down the other hallway. He saw a light in one of the classrooms. "Grandpa?" he called once again.

"What's up, J.B.?" answered Mr. Hritzay as he stepped out of the room. "Is the lock-down over?"

"Yes, Sir, and they dismissed us but told us about the pirates still being loose." he smiled and offered, "Grandpa, if you need any help today, I'm here."

"Hope you don't want to clean the art room," Mr. Hritzay chuckled.

"Been there, done that," smiled J.B.

"Well, then, I need to get work done. Hey, your mom is fixing dinner tonight and she invited me," announced his grandfather. "Tell her I'll get there on time!"

"Will do, Grandpa! See ya!" J.B. left the room.

Walking down the hall, he wondered where those awful pirates would show their faces. "I'm gonna take the long way home tonight. Maybe I'll run into them, and if that's the case, I'd better have a plan on how to catch them."

"Hey, J.B., where did you disappear to?" a voice came from behind him.

He turned. "Oh, hi, Wayne. Well, I was just thinking. We've got big trouble if we don't find those pirates and return them to the time portal."

"Yeah, so are we going to hunt for them?" asked Wayne.

"Well, sort of...I'm going home the long way."

"You mean through the park?" wondered Wayne.

"Uh huh. Come on, let's go," urged J.B.

The boys left the school and walked for a while in silence, each lost in his own thoughts. Keeping to the cedar bark trail, J.B. looked at every potential hiding spot for the two pirates. Seeing nothing strange or amiss, he motioned for Wayne to follow him.

Turning off the trail, he slid between two huge rocks. The ground sloped down a rocky path to the pond. He stood surveying the peaceful scene.

"Boy, I always like it here. Before Dad died, we'd come down and skip stones." His voice grew quiet and sad.

"You still miss your dad, don't you?" asked Wayne.

"Yeah, I'll always miss him," replied J.B. wistfully. "Mom says he's watching us from heaven. I don't know, but I hope so." He skipped a stone across the water.

"J.B.," cried Wayne, "what's that?" He pointed to a black shape floating in the water.

"Hey, it's a hat." He walked to the edge of the water and paused. "Good grief! look--it's a pirate hat! I knew it! They must be around here. Probably hiding." He reached down and retrieved the hat from the water. "Look at the blue paint on it! Man, those kindergarteners really blasted them with paint. Wayne, you don't see anything else strange here, do you? I don't."

"Nah--hey, we'd better get going," answered Wayne.

"Oh, yeah! My grandpa is coming for supper. Mom's gonna wonder what happened to me."

The friends climbed back up through the rocks to the main trail and soon reached the park gate. Two more blocks and J.B. walked down the driveway to his home while Wayne continued to his own house.

"Hey, J.B.!" a voice called from above.

Looking up, J.B. saw Tehya up in a tree, her feet dangling.

"Hey, Tehya, are you supposed to be up that high?" his voice was laced with concerned.

"No, but it's sure a good view of the streets!" laughed Tehya. "I'm watching for pirates!"

"Haven't you seen enough of them today?" teased J.B.

"Yeah, but my dad always says to be ready for opportunities." Tehya smiled. "You never know."

He smiled back at the spirited little girl. "Come on down, now. I'm sure you can watch for pirates on the ground." J.B. held out his hand to help her descend.

Safely on the ground, Tehya turned and ran toward her home, yelling, "Happy hunting, J.B."

J.B. walked into his house and was greeted nervously by his mom.

"Hi, Son, how was school today? I hear there was another emergency."

"Yeah. Those guys dressed as pirates are still around," he answered. His hand tightened around the black pirate hat he held crumpled in his hand, hoping she wouldn't notice.

His mother looked at her watch and said, "Your grandfather will be here soon. I'd better check on supper." She turned and walked into the kitchen.

10
CLUES AND NEWS

J.B. walked to his room and placed the pirate hat on his desk. "Boy, I've gotta find these two guys, get them out of this time period and back to their own world." He stared out the window. Everything appeared normal.

"I'm here," came his grandpa's voice down the hall.

J.B. realized his grandfather had just arrived. He closed his bedroom door and hurried down the hall. "Hey, Grandpa! Ready for dinner?"

"I'm as hungry as a shark!" joked Mr. Hritzay.

"Dad, son., come into the kitchen." Mrs. McBride's voice drifted through the room along with the smells of dinner.

"Coming," replied the two in unison.

Sitting down at the table, J.B. smiled at the aroma of chicken and biscuits. "Mom, I just love chicken and biscuits! Thanks for making them."

"Same here," agreed Mr. Hritzay. "Your mother would be so proud of your cooking!"

"Thanks, Dad. Thanks, J.B. I knew you'd enjoy supper." She beamed with joy.

The three settled down to enjoy their supper. The conversation was lively, discussing work and school. It finally centered on the pirates.

"Dad, what is the deal about those guys on the loose? It gives me the creeps!" shuddered J.B.'s mom.

"Well, apparently they're two bums that were passing through. The police said they would patrol the area closely tonight. It will give all the residents a sense of security. They really think they're just pranksters. There was a report of them stealing cookies from an Amish family's home. I guess the Amish missus gave one a pretty good rap on the head with a rolling pin!" He chuckled. "I bet that pirate has a headache!"

J.B. laughed, "That's soooo funny, Grandpa!"

"Well, I certainly hope we'll see or hear no more about those thugs. I hope they're history," stated Mrs. McBride.

Mr. Hritzay wiped his mouth and slowly stood up. "Well, Laurie, that was one great meal. Thank you! I have to return to school to finish buffing a floor. Both of you take care and watch out for pirates!" He laughed and walked out the door.

"Thanks for supper, Mom. Do you need help cleaning up?" asked J.B.

"How thoughtful of you," replied his mom. "But no. Go enjoy outside. You're only young once. Go play. Just be sure to stay in the neighborhood and watch out for strangers."

"Thanks, mom. See you later!" yelled J.B. as he ran out the door.

Running down the steps, his leg feeling much better, he looked across the yard to the neighbors' place. He saw Tehya digging a hole in the back yard. Walking over he asked, "Tehya, what are you doing?"

"Digging a trap," she confided.

"For what?" he wondered.

"For pirates--I want to catch them." Looking very serious, she continued, "They scare children and old people. They must be stopped."

"Does your dad know you're doing this?" asked J.B.

"Yes, he does," answered Tehya's father walking through the yard. He smiled and handed Tehya a smaller shovel. "Here, this is a Tehya sized shovel. This will work better. I'll come out and check later. I'm in the garage if you need me."

"Thanks, Dad. I'm gonna build the best pirate trap you ever saw!" her face beamed. "I'll be ready for pirates!"

"Hey, good luck. See ya!" J.B. nodded to Tehya and her father.

He walked down the driveway to the street and saw someone riding a bicycle. He recognized Wayne and waved to him. Wayne coasted into the driveway.

"O.K., J.B., did you come up with a plan?"

"No, not really, but I do know the police are beefing up security around here tonight. Gramps told me," he replied.

"We're gonna have to hide from police as well as hunt pirates?" asked Wayne.

J.B. shook his head.

"Well, let's scout around the neighborhood and plan," proposed Wayne. He paused, looking at J.B.'s leg. "How's your leg?"

"Oh, a lot better, but I forgot to feed my dog. Come on." He motioned Wayne to the backyard and stopped to grab some dog food out of the storage can.

"Rue!" called J.B. as he opened the kennel gate and both boys stepped in. A black and white face appeared out of the doghouse.

"Boy, she's sure a pretty dog," said Wayne, petting the blue-eyed husky.

"Yes, she is," agreed J.B., "but she's not a good watch dog. She always watches strange things but never barks. She's awful strong. She can pull two stone weights. Just give her a treat and she'll pull anything!" He filled her dish with food, laughed and patted her head. Rue licked his hand.

"O.K., chores done." J.B. gave Rue one more pat on the head and walked with Wayne down the driveway. Waving to Tehya, who was still digging, they started down the street. They traversed three streets. Nothing was different. All appeared normal.

"Let's walk down to the dime store," suggested J.B.

11 OUTWITTED!

"Tall John, where are we going to hide now?" demanded One Eye nervously." It's getting dark."

"Somewhere by some brick buildings," growled Tall John. "We've got to find that building with the tunnel. Why these people build so many of them I'll never know." He shook his head.

Turning down a pathway, Tall John spotted another group of trees. "Here, let's go among these trees. Come nightfall we'll go exploring again."

"I'm starving," complained One Eye.

"So am I. Do you want to go and visit that wild woman again?" joked Tall John.

"Nooooo!" One Eye responded, rubbing his head. "I still have a bump on my head from that visit. But she did make good cookies."

The pirates sat down on a fallen tree. The light became dim. Dusk was drawing near. Several minutes passed by. The pirates could barely make out the shapes of the trees. It was dark.

"O.K.," whispered Tall John, "let's go." He stood up and scuddled along the tree line. He pointed to the light ahead. "Well, those people have their torches lit."

Stealthily the pirates walked toward the lights.

Returning empty handed from their walk, J.B. and Wayne walked through the yard. Glancing next door, J.B. was surprised to see Tehya covering her hole with grass.

Noticing J.B. and Wayne, she pointed, "See, I dug down a little and Dad came and helped me. Now I'm covering the hole. Boy, will it surprise the pirates if they walk over here!" She laughed. "Then they won't be scaring any children or old people!"

The boys checked out her carefully camouflaged hole.

"Nice job, Tehya," J.B. complimented her.

Tehya threw the last bunch of grass on the hole. "There--finished! Bye guys!" She ran through the yard to join her dad in the garage.

J.B. laughed hard and crowed, "Boy, that little girl is determined. She never gives up! Hope her trap works!"

"Maybe to catch a rabbit," chuckled Wayne. "Say, it's getting dark. My mom told me to get home before then. See you tomorrow, J.B." Wayne grabbed his bike and sped toward home.

J.B. sat on the back porch gazing at the first evening star. "Gee, I wish Dad was here to help me trap these pirates," he thought out loud. He smiled, thinking of all the good times they had shared. He laughed, remembering what his dad used to say about setting plans. "Have plan A, then plan B, and if all else fails, plan C and stick to it!" He repeated the plans again. "A, B, and C, got it!"

He heard Rue growling. Looking over to her corner of the yard, he saw her staring at the bushes.

"Oh, Rue, it's probably the neighbor's cat you hear. Be a good watch dog!" He got up and opened the back door to the house. Looking back to Rue, he shook his head and walked inside.

Tall John heard something growling. He froze in his tracks.

One Eye looked around. "What was that?" he asked nervously.

"Something growling and it wasn't my stomach," muttered Tall John.

"Look over there. It looks like some houses," whispered One Eye.

"Right, Mate," agreed Tall John, peering over the bushes. "I don't see any animals or anything. Let's sneak through."

He gripped his sword and crept forward. The bushes crackled as both pirates stepped between them into the open.

"I can hardly see anything," grumbled One Eye.

"Aye, then watch where you walk," retorted Tall John.

An ominous growl filled the night air. "Steady--where is that sound coming from? It doesn't sound good," whispered One Eye.

"It's coming from a small building over there. Stay over here in this other flat place," cautioned Tall John. "Look, there are two buildings here with torches. That fence is separating them. The growl sound is on the other side of the fence--let it stay over there."

A barking dog in the distance startled the two men.

"Whale blubber! I don't like the sounds of that wolf. I hope there's not any around here. I'd rather face three sharks than a wolf!" Tall John muttered and gripped his sword tighter.

"Hey, this ground is much better to walk.....hey, help!" yelled One Eye.

"One Eye, where'd ya go?" Tall John started to speak and stepped forward. Suddenly the ground under his feet caved in. Thud! He landed on something squishy. Reaching down to touch the mass, he realized it was One Eye. "One Eye? One Eye? Wake up!" croaked Tall John, shaking the downed pirate.

"Ahh, what happened?" whined One Eye. "I was walking and boom! The ground caved away."

"Fish spit! We just walked into a hole!" Tall John's voice was filled with disgust.

They both heard movement and another growl, this time much closer. A chain began to rattle. Barking filled the quiet night. It reached a crescendo, then turned into a high pitched howl.

"Oh, sea serpents!" spat tall John. "It's a wolf, I tell you. We're trapped in a hole and a wolf is coming!" He fumbled in the dark for his sword. Tripping over One Eye, he bashed his head on the side of the hole. "Quick, find me sword! Or where is your sword?" he yelled at One Eye.

"Don't know. Can't find it!" answered One Eye.

J.B. had just settled into bed when he heard Rue barking. "She never barks at anything important," he thought. "She'll stop." But Rue continued barking and then started to howl. "Oh, great! She'll wake up the neighbors. I'd better find out what the problem is."

He got up from bed, grabbed his jacket and flashlight, and tiptoed down the hall. Stopping briefly at his mom's room, he saw she was fast asleep. "Oh, good, I don't want her to worry."

Quietly he slipped down the stairs. Rue was still howling. J.B. quickly opened the back door and stepped outside on the back porch. Shining the flashlight across the yard, he saw Rue standing stiffly in her kennel. She was barking and howling at something in the neighbor's yard.

"Rue, Rue," J.B. whispered, running across the yard to the dog. "Quiet, girl. You'll wake all the neighbors!" Rue stopped howling but her eyes stayed riveted toward Tehya's house.

"Hey, girl, is that cat bothering you?" he asked. He opened the kennel door. Rue pushed J.B. and the door.

Rue growled and J.B. could feel her hair sticking up. "Rue, is something there?" Now it was his turn to be scared. He heard thudding noises. Rue growled. Suddenly she ducked under his arm and ran straight toward the neighbor's backyard! Approaching the fence, Rue jumped it and disappeared from sight!

"Hey, wait, Rue!" J.B. crawled over the fence. The dog stood beside Tehya's pirate trap, growling!

"Now, Rue, what is so interesting?" He leaned over the hole and his mouth dropped open when his flashlight revealed what Tehya's trap held. One Eye and Tall John blinked nervously at the glare.

"Well, well, well, now it's my turn to bully except I'm not going to bully." He took one step closer to the hole. His foot hit something. Tall John's sword lay on the ground. J.B. picked it up. He held the sword, pointing the tip toward the pirates. "You're going back to your own place in time."

"Me sword, me sword! Gimme my sword!" yelled Tall John.

"Your sword? Not on your life! Finders keepers! And hush up--you'll wake the whole neighborhood!" he advised sternly.

Rue growled some more and bared her teeth. Both Tall John and One Eye cowered back in the hole.

"Rue, back off," commanded J.B. She obediently backed up and sat down on her haunches. "I guess you are a pretty good watch dog when important things happen. Good girl!" He patted Rue on the head.

"O.K., now for plan B. Rue, stay here and guard the pirates. Don't let them out of your sight. If they try to run, go for their throats!"

He glared at One Eye and Tall John to make sure they got the message. "Don't move a muscle or she'll get you. I'll be right back!"

He ran to the fence, climbed over, and slipped into his house. Quietly he picked up the phone and called Wayne. A sleepy Wayne answered.

J.B. whispered into the phone, "Wayne, get over here quick! The trap worked! I have two pirates. Rue has turned into a dog hero and she's watching them right now. We've got to get them back to the school! Hurry!" He put the phone down. Opening the closet door, he grabbed some clothesline and ran outside.

J.B. ran across the yard, scaled the fence, and found Rue patiently standing guard, a leather pouch in her jaws.

"Good, girl, Rue!" he patted her head and stuffed the pouch into his pocket. Looking around he glimpsed One Eye's sword on the ground. "Great! Now both Wayne and I will have a weapon to control these two."

The dog turned her head toward the street. Wayne slid into the driveway on his bike.

"I don't believe it! That pirate trap worked! Good for Tehya! That's such a big help! That has saved us hours of hunting."

"Well, let's get them out of the hole and tie them up. Rue will help us, but we've got to get to the time portal!" J.B. explained with a smile.

"Now maybe our lives will go back to normal," Wayne adding, grinning.

12 THE PROMISE

Tying the clothesline to the fence post, J.B. handed the rope to Tall John in the hole. "Don't try anything funny or I'll let Rue get you!" he warned.

"Keep the wolf away from me! Keep it away!" pleaded Tall John, his eyes filled with terror.

J.B. winked at Wayne. "You know the wolf hasn't eaten today, so she's good and hungry!"

Pulling Tall John to his feet, the boys quickly wrapped and tied a shorter piece of clothesline around his wrists. Wayne pulled out a roll of duct tape from his pocket.

"What's that for?" inquired J.B. as he lowered the clothesline to One Eye.

"Oh, I don't know. I've seen people use it in the movies. I thought I'd bring it to keep them quiet." He tore off a piece and covered Tall John's mouth. "There! That's effective. He won't whine about the she wolf." He laughed. He ripped off another piece of duct tape and taped One Eye's mouth once he was out of the hole.

"Let's get ready to go. Everyone is tied up. Wayne, do you see any police cruisers nearby?" asked J.B.

"Oh, I saw lights coming over, but I hid. It's after midnight and I knew it would look suspicious if a kid was running around at this hour," Wayne answered.

"Good. Then we'll stay on the streets unless we see lights and take to hiding in back yards," he replied.

"Boy, I'm glad I know who has dogs and who doesn't," added Wayne.

"Let's go," ordered J.B., putting his flashlight in his pocket and picking up Tall John's sword. "Wayne, get your sword, and between Rue and us we'll keep Tall John and One Eye walking."

Quietly the foursome walked down the driveway. J.B. glanced at his watch. "Well, it's 1 a.m. Hopefully we'll get this problem solved within the next hour."

The scuffle of feet on pavement was the only sound along Pearl Street. Rue walked beside the pirates, her nose on Tall John's leg. J.B. walked in the front and Wayne brought up the rear. Occasionally a barking dog was heard in the otherwise calm night. Turning the street corner, J.B. saw car lights coming down the street.

"Police!" he whispered. Quickly they and Rue ushered the pirates behind a house until the car drove past.

"Only one more block, then to the school," muttered Wayne. "Oh, by the way, how are we going to get into the school?"

"Oh, brother! I forgot that Grandpa has the keys," moaned J.B.

"Well, we can't break in. The school has an alarm system. We'll get caught," warned Wayne.

"Great! Here, hide behind Mrs. McAdoo's house. Stay put and I'll run over to get the keys from Gramps," decided J.B.

"Boy, are we lucky your grandpa lives nearby or we'd be in trouble," murmured Wayne.

Finding a secure place to hide behind Mrs. McAdoo's, J.B. told Wayne, "Stay here with Rue and guard them. I'll be back in a jiffy."

He took off running to his grandpa's house. Taking shortcuts through back yards, he was able to make good time. Going to the back door of his granddad's, he quietly pushed the screen from the window. Placing the screen on the ground, he carefully climbed through the window and crept through the kitchen to the key holder on the wall. When he tried to fetch out his flashlight, it was gone! "Oh no," he thought, "it must have fallen out!"

Using the dim light from the microwave display, he looked carefully through the keys and took the bunch marked "school".

He retraced his steps through the kitchen and crawled through the window. Replacing the screen, he took off running across the yard and jogged down the street, watching for any police cars. Seeing none, he sprinted down the three blocks to where he had left Wayne and the pirates.

"Got them!" he cried triumphantly. "Let's go."

Wasting no time, the group entered the school yard. "Let's try the back entrance," suggested J.B.

Car lights suddenly appeared on the side street.

"Oh, no, not now! Hide!" whispered Wayne.

The boys pushed the two pirates behind the dumpster.

"Rue!" whispered J.B. "Come here!"

Car lights shone on the dumpster. "Oh, no, Rue! Go run!" J.B. gave his dog a push. Rue ran across the parking lot.

"Copy--only a loose dog. Everything's clear," the boys heard the officer report on the radio. The police car pulled out of the parking lot and headed slowly down the street.

"That was too close," breathed J.B. The friends emerged from behind the dumpster.

Pushing Tall John and One Eye, they approached the back door. Taking the keys, J.B. quickly opened the door. Brandishing his sword, he walked in first. Light from a street lamp leaked in through the windows.

"Don't turn on the lights. We'll have to hope the street lights will give us enough light to see," remarked J.B.

Safely inside, J.B. poked his head out the door and whistled for Rue. The husky bounded over to J.B. wagging her tail.

"Thanks, girl, you saved the day in more ways than one." He held her by the collar and coaxed her inside. Rue ran over to Tall John and One Eye, growling. The fearful look in their eyes was enough for J.B. to know Rue had them under control.

"This way, follow me," Wayne instructed everyone. They walked by the office; security lights illuminated the stairway.

"Good, this helps," noted J.B. Reaching the top of the stairs, he cried, "Boy, we're almost done!" He checked his watch. "Almost 2 a.m."

The group arrived at the art room door. Walking in, J.B. said, "Man, I wish I hadn't lost my flashlight somewhere along the way!"

"Never fear," exclaimed Wayne. "When I got the duct tape, I also brought this." He help up a flashlight. "I'm a Boy Scout!" he stated proudly. "Always prepared!"

J.B. grinned and opened the closet door. "Come on, let's get this done. Help me push."

He and Wayne pushed and the wall slid open. A gust of wind blew through. Tall John mumbled something. Rue stood behind him and growled.

"You're first." Wayne pushed One Eye into the tunnel. Tall John was next with Rue glued to his side. J.B. was last to enter. Shining the flashlight, Wayne moved swiftly through the tunnel.

Ten minutes passed and the tunnel turned. The blinking green lights lit the dark space.

"We're here. Wayne, go first," ordered J.B.

Wayne stepped ahead into nothingness. Tall John, One Eye, Rue, and J.B. disappeared. The pounding of surf was a welcome sound to the boys and the pirates. Wayne reached over and yanked the duct tape off of Tall John and One Eye's mouths.

"The *Black Shark*!" yelled Tall John. "There it is."

One Eye shouted, "The Jolly Roger waves!"

Rue ran on to the beach, barking and chasing the sea gulls.

"Aye, the she wolf! Keep her away from me!" cried Tall John as Rue came bounding back to her master.

"Well, gentlemen, here's where we part company. Get away from the island and don't come back!" commanded J.B..

He untied their hands and together he, Wayne, and Rue chased the pirates through the sand. The husky ran ahead and nipped Tall John on the rump. Screaming, Tall John sprinted ahead of One Eye and jumped into the small rowboat. He grabbed the oars, waving them at Rue. One Eye ran into the water and pushed the boat into deep water. Jumping in, he and Tall John lost no time rowing away from the shore. The dog leaped into the water and swam alongside the boat.

J.B. watched as they rowed out. He yelled to Rue and she swam back, a small piece of cloth held tight in her jaws.

"Well, Rue, I see you said your good-byes in a nice way!" He started laughing and Wayne joined in. Taking the cloth from the husky's mouth, he tossed it on the sand.

"Hey, J.B.!" yelled Wayne, standing by the time portal. "Come on, let's go! It might be daylight here, but it's still 2 a.m. our time. Come on!"

J.B. turned to look at the *Black Shark* one more time. A flash of white on the deck of the ship caught his eye. "Hey, look!" he exclaimed, pointing to the ship. "Someone's waving something white!"

Rue walked over to him., whining, looking out toward the ship.

"J.B., come on! I'm tired of pirates! I want to go home! Come on!" cried Wayne impatiently.

J.B. stood staring at the ship. Suddenly he remembered, "Wayne, that little cabin boy we saw on the ship--he's still there! What about him?"

"So what if it's him? That's his problem, not ours. We can't save everyone! Let's go!" retorted Wayne.

J.B. looked sadly at the ship. Shaking his head, he turned and walked toward the time portal. He glanced wistfully at the ship again. Suddenly he smiled. Reaching into his pocket he took out his red bandanna. Tying it on the branches of a bush, he gazed at the ship. "I'll come back to rescue you, I promise."

He then took Rue by the collar, walked to the time portal and disappeared into nothingness.

The wind blew across the beach; the red bandanna waved in the breeze as if saying farewell.

— EPILOGUE—

Safely returning from the time portal, J.B., Rue, and Wayne returned to their homes.

Tehya found an empty trap the next morning. Running to her dad, she told him about her find.

"Well, did you find any treasures?" inquired her father.

"No, let's check," replied Tehya.

Together father and daughter walked out to the hole. Bending down, Tehya picked up something dark from the ground.

"Look, Dad! It's a hat." She put it on her head. "A pirate hat! They were here!" she said excitedly.

"And now they're gone," said J.B., standing by the fence, smiling, a small leather pouch clutched in his hand.

CPSIA information can be obtained at www.ICGtesting.com
Printed in the USA
BVOW042144100413

317856BV00008B/204/P